"Put it out [...] Reece sai[d]

Bella shook her head. "So, as far as Strong Nation Holdings is concerned, Harrison's Food Shop can sink or swim?"

"Look," he said, "you can't have it both ways. Either you agree to my proposition or you don't." She shook her head again. "You don't. So stop making provocative remarks."

He looked down at her, eyes hooded. "You threw my coat back at me when it rained. You stood me up in the middle of a dance at Jacqueline's party. There's a limit to what a man—let alone a businessman—can take."

For some reason, Bella had to go on fighting this man who was her enemy, even though her other self was saying, Enough is enough—for heaven's sake, be quiet.

LILIAN PEAKE lives near the sea in England. Her first job was working for a mystery writer, employment that she says gave her an excellent insight into how an author functions. She went on to become a journalist and reported on the fashion world for a trade magazine. Later she took on an advice column, the writing of which contributed to her understanding of people's lives. Now she draws on her experiences and perception, not to mention a fertile imagination, to craft her many fine romances. She and her husband, a college principal, have three children.

Books by Lilian Peake

HARLEQUIN PRESENTS

HARLEQUIN ROMANCE

Don't miss any of our special offers. Write to us at the following address for information on our newest releases.

Harlequin Reader Service
P.O. Box 1397, Buffalo, NY 14240
Canadian address: P.O. Box 603,
Fort Erie, Ont. L2A 5X3

LILIAN PEAKE

irresistible enemy

Harlequin Books

TORONTO • NEW YORK • LONDON
AMSTERDAM • PARIS • SYDNEY • HAMBURG
STOCKHOLM • ATHENS • TOKYO • MILAN
MADRID • WARSAW • BUDAPEST • AUCKLAND

Harlequin Presents first edition August 1992
ISBN 0-373-11485-0

Original hardcover edition published in 1990
by Mills & Boon Limited

IRRESISTIBLE ENEMY

CHAPTER ONE

'I'M GLAD your father could spare you for half an hour,' Jacqueline remarked, stirring her coffee and addressing her friend across the table.

'So am I,' Bella answered, spreading with jam and cream the scone she couldn't really afford. 'But we're not exactly rushed off our feet in the shop. Trade hasn't been very brisk lately, to put it mildly. Of course, our long-time customers stick with us, but...' She turned down her mouth, then curved it again to accommodate the bite as she sank her small white teeth into the tasty confection.

'It's months since we've met, isn't it?' Jacqueline commented, drinking some coffee. 'It's seemed a long time, especially as in our youth——' she laughed at her own remark '—well, you know, when we were schoolkids, we used to see each other every day.'

In those days, Bella remembered, Jacqueline, dark-haired, brown, laughing eyes, had been the only member of the wealthy Strangor-Denman family to acknowledge the existence of Isabella Harrison from the other end of the town. From time to time, one or other of them had come into her parents' grocery store.

Whereas Jacqueline had chatted and laughed and even at times, climbed the steps to the Harrisons' apartment above the shop, her parents and her brother, if they had ever deigned to enter the store, would purchase their groceries and walk out without a word, or even a smile, even though Bella herself, her chestnut hair tamed into pigtails, might have been serving in order to help her parents out.

Correction, she thought, pressing a reflective finger on to crumbs scattered over her plate, Reece Strangor-Denman had noticed her existence. His eyes, youthful yet deeply male, had appraised her face with its fair skin and the burgeoning figure beneath the overwashed sweaters which, through shortage of spare cash for such things as new clothes, she used to have to wear. Bella recalled how her cheeks had burned under Reece's young masculine scrutiny.

I hated him, she remembered, for his cool inspection of me, for that arrogance of his and his superior ways, for his height and his good looks, his boundless confidence—which had grown even stronger as his years at university had passed.

Yet, day after day, she had found herself looking for him, and, as weeks had gone by without a sign of him, she had been swept by a curious disappointment. What had puzzled her so much had been the way his whole demeanour had both angered and repelled her. Yet, contrariwise, she had felt herself as drawn to him as though he had twirled a lasso and caught her, pulling her relentlessly towards him.

'The main reason I wanted to see you,' said Jacqueline, extending her pink-tipped fingers, 'was to show you this.'

'You're engaged! I'm so glad for you. It's a beautiful ring, Jacqueline,' Bella enthused. 'Is it Dick Fowler?'

'It is.' Jacqueline's happiness shone through. 'He's a great guy, Bella. I only wish you could find someone as good as he is,' she added with a happy sigh.

Bella laughed. 'One day, maybe. But I'm so busy helping my dad these days, there's no room, really, for any other male in my life. Apart from the occasional date, that is.'

'The other reason I wanted to meet you,' Jacqueline said, draining her cup, pushing it away and rising to join a time-conscious Bella, 'is that Dick and I are giving an engagement party at the house. We'd like you to come, Bella.' Out in the street, she squeezed Bella's arm. 'Please. For the sake of old times. No,' with a frown as memories caught up, 'for *our* sakes, I mean.'

On how many occasions, Bella tried to recollect, had Jacqueline come to tea upstairs at her parents' house adjacent to the shop?

'Don't let on to my mum and dad,' she used to say, tucking in to Bella's mother's buns and sponge cakes. 'They'd half slay me if they knew I'd been here, let alone had tea with you. But,' she'd always added, 'my mum doesn't cook like you, Mrs Harrison. She isn't so—so loving, either, or so, well, motherly.' Then Jacqueline would look around. 'I feel happy and comfortable here, somehow. Our house,' she would frown, 'it's so—you know, grand, and my dad's so pompous——'

'Hush,' Mrs Harrison used to caution, but Jacqueline would go on,

'And my mum, I love her, but—well, she...' And then Jacqueline would draw herself up at the tea table and pretend to look down her nose, first at Bella, then Bella's mother and toss her head in dismissal, at which point they would all dissolve into laughter.

'I wish, I *wish*,' Jacqueline had often said, 'I could ask you to tea, Bella, at my house. I could show you my room. I've got posters all round the walls, books and a desk to do my homework. That's one place,' she used to confess, 'where, thank heaven, my mum never pokes her nose. Reece comes in sometimes, but...'

And then she would sigh and take another bite of fruit cake.

'You will come to the party, won't you?' Jacqueline broke into Bella's thoughts. She mentioned the date.

'You mean,' Bella said, half teasing, 'you're actually inviting me, Isabella Harrison, to your parents' *house*?'

Jacqueline smiled ruefully, plainly remembering the past.

'Anyway,' Jacqueline went on, walking with Bella, 'why shouldn't you come? Reece bought it from them.'

'*Bought* it? Do you mean they *sold* the house to your brother? Isn't it usual for well-off parents to *give* their property to their offspring?'

Jacqueline smiled ruefully. 'You don't know my parents. In your world, parental affection and especially generosity—something else I remember clearly from the past...your wonderful mum and dad...yes?—is as natural within the family circle as night follows day.'

They stood together outside 'Harrison's Food Fare'. Jacqueline waved to Bella's father as he glanced out.

'I mustn't keep you, looks like your dad needs help.' Nevertheless, she added, 'Anyway, Reece has got plenty of money of his own, and he saw it as a way of making Mum and Dad financially secure for the rest of their lives. Plus acquiring a place to live, a sort of permanent base, and one he's always loved. I guess he also had marriage in mind.'

'He's engaged, then?' Bella heard a strange catch in her voice. For some obscure reason, it seemed to matter to her that Reece Strangor-Denman had a wife-to-be.

'*Engaged?*' Jacqueline laughed. 'Not yet, probably not for years, knowing him. You won't find my dear brother giving up easily his freedom of movement and choice— that is, of women. His current lady is Marguerite Hunter-Parkes. She's a dress designer. Not for your off-the-peg shoppers like you and me. Strictly for those rolling in it. By the way, Reece calls himself Denman now,' she added. 'He's dropped the Strangor bit, except for formal occasions. He thinks it makes him sound more approachable. Ha! My brother Reece, *approachable*?'

Bella laughed with her friend, but without Jacqueline's amusement. It sounded as if Reece Denman hadn't changed over the years. Even in his early twenties he had seemed to Bella a formidable creature, out of her reach—not that she had ever wanted him to be within it, she'd told herself disdainfully. She'd no more belonged to his world then than she did now. Nor would she ever.

'Know anyone to bring? To the party, I mean,' Jacqueline asked, preparing to leave. 'A partner, a bloke? We usually invite people in pairs. If not, don't worry.'

'There's Jimmy Canford, or his brother Vernon. I go out with one or the other occasionally.'

'Hey, two men at your beck and call?' Jacqueline exclaimed, laughing. 'You believe there's safety in numbers? You dark horse, Bella Harrison, especially as you told me you're too busy to bother about having a male in your life. If you can't make up your mind which one to ask,' she teased, 'bring them both. See you.'

Two evenings later, Bella parked the car on a verge, half on and half off the road, making sure it was securely locked. Not that the car was an up-to-date model, nor was it in tip-top condition, but as a vehicle it was as valuable to her father and herself as a Rolls-Royce to a rich man.

With it, they made their weekly grocery deliveries, a feature of Harrison's personal service that her father had insisted on keeping on in the face of the formidable competition which came from supermarket shopping.

'So everyone collects their own goods these days,' he had said. 'There are plenty who can't, aren't there, like the elderly, the disabled and those too hard up to own cars?'

Bella scanned with her usual pleasure the panorama of hedges and green fields, the countryside she loved. It was spring; it was evening. So what if there were a few clouds in the sky, threatening to encroach on the sunset? She had the rest of the day to herself, a time she treasured.

Her feet, despite her having been on them all day, tugged at her body like an eager dog at his lead. Walk, they said, and every evening, especially on Saturdays with Sunday ahead, she gladly obeyed their command.

Following the path, she branched away to cross the field, making for the stile. This Bella climbed on to, and stood, hands in pockets, surveying the view. The wind caught at her rich chestnut curls, flinging them playfully over her oval-shaped face. There below was Windhamleigh, where she had been born, and where her parents had lived since their marriage many years before.

By straining her eyes in the glow from the sunset, she could just pick out the road where her father's shop stood. Her gaze swung to the other side of the town, the 'richer' side where the better-off lived, the more privileged section of the town's population. Where Reece Strangor-Denman lived, along with Jacqueline and their wealthy parents.

So hard had Bella been staring into the distance that she had failed to notice the tall, striding figure coming towards her from out of the gathering dusk. With a shock, she focused on it.

Many times she had walked that way, and across other fields, too. Never before had she felt the slightest stirring of fear at meeting a stranger, not even when that stranger was male. Now a curious foreboding gripped her and, although she stayed where she was, panic rose inside her, but still something kept her there, hands clenched in pockets, hair tossing everywhere.

'Run,' shouted a voice in her head. 'Run now while there's still time. Get out of that man's path and back to the safety of your car.'

He wore a dark brown high-collared jacket, its zip unfastened, while his hands were hidden in its pockets. His trousers were fawn and taut, the legs pushed into wellington boots.

His black hair was wind-tossed, fanning out to cover his forehead. He was closer now; Bella picked out his features, high cheekbones and long, no-nonsense nose, eyebrows that dipped low, then ended in an unexpected and decidedly quizzical arch.

She knew him! So she could relax, couldn't she? But the tension inside her mounted rather than lessened. He was advancing towards her from out of the past. He was nearer now, and she stood her ground, intending to jump down at the last moment and let him go, pretending she did not recognise him.

Panic had receded, but a strange emotional turbulence persisted, as if a sense beyond her conscious knowledge was telling her that the necessity to turn and run from this man was greater than ever before.

He came to a halt in front of her, half of him plainly irritated by the barrier she presented to his progress, the other half regarding her with surprised interest.

Bella knew she should step down from the stile, but something kept her stubbornly fixed to the spot. A curious sense of triumph filled her. For the first time in her life, she felt superior to this chauvinistic male. She was forcing Reece Strangor-Denman to look *up* to her. Now, he just *had* to acknowledge her existence.

'Want some help in getting down?' he asked briskly, as the wind moved in little eddies around them. Was he hoping, she wondered, that it would blow her away?

'No, thanks,' she answered with a tight little smile, tossing her hair to move the straying curls from across her eyes.

He frowned, considering her. 'Isabella Harrison.'

'You remember, then?' She was as surprised as her voice implied. She hadn't thought her name would figure in the current account of Reece Strangor-Denman's verbal cash columns, let alone linger for so long in his memory bank. Had it, she wondered, earned interest there? Or lost it?

'Oh, yes. I remember. How could I forget?' The satirical note told Bella that, without doubt, in his eyes her value over the years had plummeted.

He had been attractive before, but the passage of time had added a devastating power to his bearing, broadening and strengthening it. His eyes, also, had changed. In the past they had been wide and youthfully lustful. Time had altered that, too.

Now, they were impossible to read, narrowed as they were, and estimating, as if they were assessing the depth of her sexuality and her experience in that particular sphere. She grew hot under his appraisal and wished she had not had the misfortune to meet him in this way.

Lids lowered, he raked her figure with his gaze as, defiant and challenging, her stare blazing fire, she opposed him with all her strength. Her eyes reflected the gold of the setting sun, the pale skin of her cheeks picking up the dying evening's soft-hued shades.

Her whole bearing dared him to storm her defences and, pleased now, she watched annoyance—and something else—flick across his face. It was that unreadable 'something else' that made her wonder if she should after all step down, allowing him to cross.

He solved the problem. His hands came out, delving beneath her flapping jacket, fixing hard around her slender waist and swinging her aside as easily as if she were made of cotton wool. That obstacle to his progress disposed of to his satisfaction, his hands found his pockets again. He seemed in no hurry to move on.

His show of strength angered her, for that was what it had been. Otherwise, Bella argued, wouldn't he have crossed the stile himself? Her cheeks now vied in colour with the pink and ruby splashed across the sky.

The feel of his fingers as they had clasped around her, pressing into her body so near to her breasts, had sent shock-waves around her entire system. It was the first physical contact she had ever had with him and it had shaken her to her core.

'Going somewhere?' he asked, easier in his bearing now that the opposition had been vanquished.

She answered just as succinctly, not that she could, in her present peculiar state of shock, have spoken more fluently, 'For a walk.'

He nodded, his eyes, to her annoyance, still engaged in a geographical survey of the inlets and contours of her very feminine outline. 'A lone walker?' he asked idly. 'You're a solitary creature these days?'

She let a few moments tick away before replying, wanting to wrap her wind-worried jacket around her to insulate herself from his slightly insolent appraisal of her personal statistics.

'I'm not sure,' she answered slowly, 'why you said "these days". I've never disliked my own company, either in the past or now.'

'What do you do for a living?'

Did he really want to know, she wondered, or was he merely making conversation? 'I help my father at the shop.' She lifted her head a little higher. 'I still work hard. I have to. The Harrison family, unlike the Strangor-Denmans, still don't **have a** great deal in the way of worldly goods.'

The movement of his mouth paid lip-service to a smile. 'You haven't changed. Still taking on the world. Your eyes still spit fire when they look at me.'

'Thank you kindly,' she retorted, 'for that character reference. Would you put it in writing some time so that I could use it one day to show a potential employer?'

He laughed and the world around Bella stood still, even the birds seeming for a moment to hold their breaths. What, she wondered anxiously, was the matter with her? This was only Reece Strangor-Denman, wasn't it, securely on his feet, no horse nor shining armour in sight?

'Your father OK?' Bella nodded. 'Your mother?'

Bella looked away. The subject was still painful to her. 'She died a few years ago.'

'I'm very sorry to hear that.'

Bella's head swung defensively round, but there seemed to be genuine regret in his voice.

'We miss her badly,' she added to her own surprise. Now why, she reprimanded herself, was she proceeding to pour out her heart to this cold man at one single expression of condolence?

'I'm quite sure you do.' Again no sarcasm, nor mockery in his eyes.

She cleared her throat and looked down. 'Er—my feet were made for walking.' Her smile was fleeting, there merely for convention's sake. 'If you'll excuse me...'

She made to go on, in the direction from which he had come. He moved to block her way. 'I'll go back on my tracks and walk with you.'

Panic began to rise again, the same fear as when she had first spied him, a mere striding shape in the distance. Her sixth sense which had operated at the time had been quite correct. This man, she somehow knew, was a threat to her peace of mind.

'No, thanks,' she answered as politely as she could. 'I have other people's company every day and all day through my work. Therefore, I prefer to take my evening walks alone.'

A spot descended from the skies, hitting her nose. 'Oh, no.' She rubbed at it, but another spot joined it. It had started to rain. Preoccupied as she had been with the unexpected reappearance in her life of a man she had thought she would never see again—nor, she told herself now, had she particularly wanted to—she had failed to notice how the innocent-looking cloud she had seen earlier had now spread itself with menacing intent across the pale blue of the sky. She turned to retrace her steps.

'I'll walk with you,' he repeated, leaping the stile she had just climbed over.

Barring taking to her heels in an undignified effort to escape his company, there was nothing she could do. The spots of rain grew heavier, and a downpour proceeded to wet her hair, her face and her lightweight jacket.

'Here,' he drew off his own jacket, 'borrow this.'

Before she could protest, it was draped around her shoulders. Again, she realised how childish it would look if she followed her instinct and shrugged it off until it fell to the ground.

But she didn't want its residual warmth—his bodily warmth—hugging her; nor did she want anything of his to protect her, not even from a tropical storm, let alone a mere heavy shower.

'No, thanks.' She found her shoulders moving of their own accord. 'I'm not afraid of a few drops of rain. Besides,' she looked him up and down, 'you're getting soaked now.' She reached round to free herself of its protection, its strangely exciting male scent.

He stilled her hand with his. 'Leave it.'

Bella obeyed his instruction at once, relieved to her depths when he removed his hand from hers.

'I'll survive,' he countered drily, strolling beside her, hands in pockets as if the evening were still as fine as when they had both started on their separate walks.

'Do you still live over the shop?' he asked, his dark, short-sleeved shirt slowly becoming plastered to his chest and broad shoulders, although he seemed unaware of the fact.

'Yes. What's wrong with that?' She heard the aggression in her own voice. 'I like my side of the town. It's where I feel happiest. If anyone offered me a place on *your* side of the town, I wouldn't accept it, even if it were rent-free.'

'Wow. Does that mighty chip on your shoulder weigh you down?'

She heard the sarcasm but decided to ignore it. Instead, she fished for her car keys, opening the door and sliding behind the wheel.

Turning at last to look up at him, she saw the rain running in rivulets down his face, his hair flattened to his head, his shirt clinging to the muscular torso. She had a frightening and completely alien urge to protect him with her own body, to shield him from the elements, to tell him to beware, in case he caught a chill.

Why, she asked herself a little desperately, should his plight arouse such a surge of warmth inside her? Why should she be swept by a strange compassion, and why should it all be mixed in with a curious fear? What was happening to her? No matter what, she mustn't even begin to like this man, let alone experience a stronger emotion for him.

'I——' She cleared her throat that was oddly tight. 'I could give you a lift.'

'Thanks for the offer, but rain or not I'd prefer to walk.' No explanation, just a blunt, dismissing refusal.

'So,' she heard herself fling at him, 'it's beneath your dignity, is it, to travel in the Harrisons' car, old and shabby as it is, the one we use to make deliveries with? OK, so get soaked to the skin. Why should I care, when you don't care one atom, never have, have you, for others less fortunate than yourself?'

So she'd blown her top, given way to that tearing resentment against him and his family—Jacqueline apart—which to her secret horror still seemed to lie deep and lasting within her. Now, she told herself, she was beyond caring. He shouldn't have forced his company on her, spoilt her walk...

The sight of him standing there, so very much in command of the situation, so rawly attractive in the darkened, rain-swept evening, so much beyond the reach of a girl like her who inhabited a world he so plainly despised, had goaded her beyond endurance.

The sweet, compassionate feeling his drenched appearance had started to arouse transmuted itself into an angry animal, twisting round to maul itself to pieces. She was, she realised, still wearing his jacket. Well, she would take great pleasure in giving it back to him. Her hand grabbed it from her shoulders, swinging it outwards. The garment landed unceremoniously at his feet.

A surreptitious glance at him revealed taut, angry lips. Above them were two eyes darker than the black clouds that clustered overhead.

She fired the engine and bumped back on to the road, leaving him standing there, jacket still on the ground, staring after her, a barely reigned-in fury in every line of him.

CHAPTER TWO

'BELLA, what *have* you been up to?' Jacqueline teased on the phone next day. 'Reece told me he met you out walking and you turned on him like a spitfire. "My friend Bella a *spitfire?*" I asked him. "You must be joking." But he said like hell he was. He was angry, Bella.'

'Was he?' Bella asked with false innocence, forcefully quelling a spurt of fear. 'I can't think why.'

'Listen, you watch out. Reece isn't just back in town, he intends to stay. His company's head office has moved into this area and they're currently mopping up supermarkets like there's no tomorrow.'

'That's OK,' Bella pretended a blandness she did not feel, 'we're not a supermarket, Dad and me, we're just a small corner shop, so we don't have to worry. Your brother won't be interested in us.'

'Don't be so sure. Strong Nation Holdings are big fish these days. They're stalking little fish, Bella, and swallowing them whole.'

Bella's heart lurched, but she would not admit to Jacqueline that her words had got her worried. Her friend she might be, but Jacqueline was still the sister of the man she had begun to hate.

'His wonderful company had better leave my dad's business alone,' Bella answered with feeling. 'I won't have him worried.'

'Look after him, Bella,' her friend advised sympathetically. 'He's all you've got, isn't he? And I just happen to be fond of him, too, you know. When we were schoolkids I used to look up to him, did you know that? And your mum. My own parents, well, they were so wrapped up in their own affairs they didn't have time for me, not like your—but I've told you all that before, haven't I?'

Many times, Bella thought, with a warmly reminiscent smile.

'Thanks for the warning, Jacqueline. I'll tell my dad to be on his guard against any marauding pirates who might come banging on the door threatening to take his business away!'

'Ever been to the Strangor-Denman stronghold before?' Vernon Canford asked as his much-repaired sports car coped gamely with the hill it was climbing.

He pointed its snorting nose towards the sweeping, tree-lined driveway and found a place among the odd assortment of vehicles which Jacqueline's other friends had used to convey them to her engagement celebration.

The house carried its two centuries with dignity and calm. Made of golden stone, its pointed gables jostled against brick chimneys and its mullioned windows gazed out in all directions.

'Windham House? Never,' Bella answered, gazing at the aloof-looking residence with an awe left over from childhood, mixed in with a very adult twist of resentment. 'I was never considered good enough to be invited to step over its very distinguished threshold. Not by Jacqueline's parents, anyway. I'm told it belongs to their son now,' she added.

The knowledge didn't make it any easier for her to approach the impressive residence which in the old days had, for her, possessed magic, almost secretive properties, and around which she had woven glamorous stories. The reason being, she acknowledged now, that distance lent enchantment and that, even though she was a friend of the daughter of the house, her parents' somewhat shaky financial standing had precluded her from ever taking one step inside the place.

'Phew, what a mansion!' Vernon exclaimed. 'Never seen it in close-up before. Sure your friend won't object to me being there?'

Bella laughed, squeezing Vernon's hand. 'You're every bit as good as they are. We're all the same under the skin, just people, whether we're wealthy, hard up, or in the lower middle, like you and me. Come on, let's go in.'

The door was flung open by a brilliant-eyed Jacqueline. 'Welcome to the Denman mud hut,' she cried, drawing laughter from the crowd behind her. 'Oh, is that for Dick and me? You are a dear.' She accepted the package that Bella held out to her, beckoning them inside.

Unwrapping the engagement gift, she gave a little shriek. 'Hey, Dick, love, look what Bella and Vernon have given us. A beautiful ornament, look, ceramic birds among the reeds and leaves. Aren't they Canada geese? Exactly like the ones you see in the Duke's Park. They're just great, Bella. Handmade?'

Bella nodded. 'And hand-painted. From Betty Hammond's craft shop in the town.'

'I love it, Bella, and so does Dick.' Jacqueline hugged her friend, then Vernon, first putting the ornament safely aside.

'Hey, Bella love, you look just great. That dress. Have I seen it somewhere before?'

'Yeah,' shouted a male voice from the depths of the hall, 'at the ladies' committee jumble sale.'

'Malc,' Jacqueline exclaimed angrily, 'I'll kill you! Come on in, loves, to where it's all happening.'

Bella remembered the 'Malc' Jacqueline had addressed. Malcolm Haddern was his full name. He had been a friend of Reece's all those years ago, and she had never liked him. Like Reece, he had patronised Harrison's Food Fare and let his glance linger on the young and attractive girl behind the counter. Except that his eyes had made the teenage Bella's skin crawl, whereas Reece's had made her hot and very bothered.

'Seriously,' Jacqueline eyed the neat floral print dress that Bella wore, 'I'm sure it's familiar.'

'You came with me to buy it three—er——' She almost said 'years' which would have been true.

Jacqueline, quick to understand, filled in, 'Three months ago? I remember now. Hey, Dick love, a drink for my special guests.'

Bella looked about her, glass in hand, feeling more than a little lost. She hadn't asked Jacqueline if her brother would be attending the party and she hoped he wouldn't show up.

Only on one of her recent evening walks had she seen him, and as they had approached each other Bella had trodden doggedly on. Reece had stared at the ground as though he was analysing its mineral content, while Bella's gaze had rested on him, dreading the moment when he would force her to a stop and tell her how much her action in throwing his jacket at him had angered him.

To her astonishment, and more surprising still, a curious sense of disappointent, he had raised his eyes and, finding hers still upon him, had nodded tersely and walked on.

Returning abruptly to the present, she looked at Vernon, who, at that precise moment, looked at her. It seemed he was as out of his depth as she was.

'Is this what they call high society?' Vernon asked under his breath.

'Not sure,' Bella answered. 'Spin-offs from it, more likely, you know, the junior version.'

'Isabella Harrison, well, well.' Malcolm Haddern struck a belligerent pose in front of them, glass in his hand. 'All little girls grow, they tell me, but,' his eyes went on the old familiar path over Bella's shape, 'what they didn't tell me was how *beautiful* they grow.' He looked from her to Vernon. 'One of the Canford brothers. You both still help your father run the Throttle Filling Station?'

Bella could almost feel her companion bristling. He, too, it seemed, had heard Malcolm Haddern's patronising tone, and the faint contempt in his voice. It goes, she thought angrily, with him, with the people Reece Denman mixes with.

Vernon produced a card, holding it out. 'Throttle's the best in town,' he averred, undaunted by Malcolm's manner. 'James and Vernon Canford, vehicle mechanics. If you ever want your car repaired, call on the experts.'

Malcolm took it, reading it uninterestedly.

'And are they "experts"!' Bella put in, wanting to back Vernon up in his effort to lift himself above the level of mere artisan to which Malcolm Haddern had assigned him.

At Bella's words, Malcolm turned and raised frankly insulting eyebrows towards her. 'And you should know, dear Bella, you should know. I've heard talk since I came back to the area that Isabella Harrison can often be seen with one Canford brother on each arm.'

Vernon made a jerking movement towards Malcolm but Bella's steadying hand acted as a timely restraint.

Malcolm's attention shifted. 'Hi, Reece.' He raised his glass and moved to the door.

Oh, heavens, Bella thought, Reece has come after all.

His gaze swept round, swooping to rest on her, his expression detached and cold. He appeared to have as little wish to make contact with her as she had with him. Which could only mean that he hadn't forgotten, either. Or forgiven, probably.

He glanced at Vernon, nodded in unsmiling recognition, and returned his attention to Malcolm Haddern, apparently putting Bella out of his mind.

Turning to Vernon, she commented with a forced casualness, 'The party seems to have spilt over into the garden. Let's join them, shall we?'

There was dancing on the lawn to taped and amplified music. Temporary lamps had been installed to floodlight the area and the shrubs and spring flowers blossomed and glowed, contributing to the party spirit.

Vernon, rhythm in his bones, seized Bella and drew her among the dancers. He swung and stamped, pulling Bella with him.

Drinks on laden trays moved round, ice rattled into glasses at the makeshift bar, corks popped and guests shrieked as champagne flowed freely.

Vernon seized a couple of glasses as the tray passed by, giving one to Bella, drinking between gulps of air as he regained his breath. Above bobbing heads, Bella saw Reece. He was standing with Jacqueline and Dick on the periphery of the lawn.

Jacqueline waved to Bella, who waved back. Determined to show the world and especially Reece Strangor-Denman that she was enjoying herself, she put her empty glass beside Vernon's and threw herself into the dancing.

The sky had darkened and the trees took up the song of the sighing breeze. A barbecue manned by hired caterers replaced the warmth of the vanished sun.

The cry went up, 'Food. Come and get it.' In no time, a long line had formed, plates and cutlery held out to receive the appetising portions.

Bella stood to one side with Vernon, who took big mouthfuls and looked around constantly. 'No one here

I know,' he commented at last. 'But I suppose there wouldn't be, would there?'

Reece was deep in conversation with an older man who gave a nod, put down his empty plate and made his way towards Bella and her partner.

He was smiling as he approached, nodding to Bella and speaking to Vernon. 'Mr Canford? I understand from Reece Denman that you and your brother run a vehicle repair shop?'

'We help our dad,' Vernon explained.

'Fine. Bruce Hunter-Parkes.' The newcomer shook Vernon's hand. 'You might have heard of my daughter, Marguerite. She's a top people's dress designer.' Bella nodded. 'Reece, there, he knows her well, if you get my meaning. He tells me you and your brother are experts in car maintenance. That being so——'

'Don't know about that,' Vernon put in, 'but we always do our best.'

Mr Hunter-Parkes nodded, 'That's what I'm after. Efficiency. Reece says you know it all backwards. And what's more, you're on the level.'

Vernon nodded decisively.

'Right. So I've got a proposition. My company, Hunter-Parkes Associates, market research—we run a fleet of cars. We don't like the present lot who service our vehicles, so how about you taking them on? Terms of contract good, you play fair with us, we'll treat you right, too.'

Vernon, who flushed deeply, both at the compliments and the prospect of so much good business coming Throttle's way, said with a caution Bella knew he was superimposing upon his pleasure, 'I'll certainly speak to my dad, Mr Hunter-Parkes. I'll get him to ring you.' He exchanged the proffered business card with one of his own.

'Good. I'm sure we can come to an amicable arrangement.' Bruce Hunter-Parkes nodded again and walked off.

'Hey, Bella, am I dreaming? All that new work coming our way.' Vernon hugged her and pulled her back towards the dancers, but another man, younger this time, approached, halting them.

'Been looking for you, Mr Canford. Can you spare a sec? It's about my car. Reece has recommended you.'

Vernon looked with eager expectancy at the man, then regretfully at Bella, who flapped her hand, telling him silently, Don't worry about me, seize every opportunity that comes your way.

Vernon pushed another drink into Bella's hand and went off with his potential customer. Hiding her face with the raised glass, Bella glanced secretly towards where Reece was standing. His eyes were on her and a tiny knot of tension made itself felt somewhere in the region of her stomach. What was his motive, she wondered, in sending that work Vernon's way? Well, she certainly was not going to ask him.

In case he thought she wanted his company to fill the lonesome minutes in Vernon's absence, she turned away and wandered round the corner of the house, finding a paved area shaded by blossoming shrubs.

A white table stood in its centre surrounded by empty seats. Making for the quiet corner, Bella pushed aside the assorted tumblers and glass tankards and sat down. Over the rim of her glass, she watched people passing. For the first time that evening, she began to relax her guard.

Someone approached and Bella recognised the laughing and chattering voice as Jacqueline's. Spying Bella, she shrieked delightedly, pulling away from her fiancé's possessive arm.

'Bella, dear old pal,' she sank into a chair, 'what're you doing hidden away here? And on your own, too. Where's the boyfriend?'

Bella smiled, explaining Vernon's absence. 'It's a lovely party, Jacqueline. Thanks a lot for inviting me.'

'Think nothing of it. Had to have you, my best friend.'

It was not difficult to deduce that Jacqueline had drunk only just the right side of sufficiency. 'Hey, Dick,' Jacqueline directed, 'get Bella some grub, there's a love. Where's Vernon?' she asked again.

Patiently, Bella repeated her explanation.

'Oh, business.' Jacqueline snorted. 'Can't have you sitting alone at my engagement party. Thanks a million, darling,' as her fiancé appeared with an overflowing plate, pushing it towards Bella. 'Hey, Reece,' as he came into view, 'do your duty, dear brother, and keep my best friend company.'

'Jacqueline, no!' Bella exclaimed, adding hurriedly at her friend's puzzled frown, 'I really meant, I'm quite happy here. Vernon will be back soon——'

But Jacqueline paused only to urge her brother into the seat she had vacated.

'Please don't feel under an obligation to keep me company, Mr Denman,' Bella said at once. 'Your sister press-ganged you into this, which wasn't fair, so——'

Ignoring her outburst, he forked food into his mouth from the plate he had brought. For a few moments Bella watched him, and found herself wondering how a man of his lean physique could have such an excellent appetite yet remain so untroubled by excess weight. Then she looked at the appetising mixture on her own plate.

His was emptying fast.

'You——' She felt her mouth watering. 'You look hungry,' she commented to ease the tension between them. At least, she thought, *I'm* tense, even if he isn't, and, on glancing at him again, she could tell that he was not.

'I was, Miss Harrison,' he replied laconically, pushing away his plate and leaning back. 'I did the sensible thing and satisfied my appetite. Why,' his voice had softened subtly, 'don't you do likewise?'

The miniature lights overhead shed an intriguing glow over her companion's features. He leaned forward, resting his arms on the table. By his enigmatic gaze, Bella took a guess as to which kind of 'appetite' he had in mind. The thought made her go cold, then caused a strange and disconcerting warmth to flow through her.

His face was nearer than it had ever been, just across the small table. Now that he had changed his position, the parasol above them threw his face into a tantalising half-shadow, giving a mystery to his eyes, and keeping the secrets of his smile.

As if mesmerised she picked up her fork and did as he had suggested. After a while, she pushed her plate away, taking a drink of the wine Dick had brought along with the food. She looked down into the glass, saw within its golden liquidity the reflection of the coloured lights.

'I'm sorry,' she heard herself say, the words speaking themselves because she certainly hadn't given them permission, 'for throwing your jacket back at you the other evening.'

It was as if Reece had been turned to stone, he sat so still, his eyes glinting with a mysterious inner light.

The music beyond the shrubbery which surrounded the patio came to a stop.

'That apology,' he said huskily, rising and coming to stand behind her, 'must have cost Isabella Harrison a great deal, proud as she is and hating me as she does.'

'But I don't——' she was about to say, but she halted the denial in its tracks. 'And I'm not proud,' she added indignantly.

Reece leaned forward and fixed the upper section of the parasol at an angle, thus concealing them from the rest of the world. His fingers reached forward and he tipped her face. She saw his lips descending, slowly, surely. There would have been time to evade them, to twist away and cry 'No!' but all her reflexes were locked into the receiving mode. Her lips had taken a vote between themselves and decided unanimously that they wanted the kiss that was coming her way!

His mouth made contact, upside-down, cool and assured. The kiss in its very lightness was both tender and erotic and, as it repeated itself twice more, left those wayward lips of hers tremulous and wilful and asking for more.

Reece laughed. It was low and rumbling and Bella could feel its vibrations against the back of her head.

'Enough of that kind of sound,' someone shouted as if from a great distance. 'Let's change the mood. Mozart while we eat. OK, everybody? Get ready for the culture shock.'

'Culture with a capital "K",' joked a voice which Bella recognised as that of Malcolm Haddern. 'You know, k-u-l-c-h-e-r,' he deliberately misspelt the word, 'such as our sweet little shop assistant Bella Harrison would spell it.'

'And her grease-stained car mechanic of a boyfriend,' someone took him up.

'Which one?' another voice answered. 'There are two of them, and they're both grease-stained.'

'Hey, fellas,' it was Malcolm again, 'that girl must have something out of this world if she can keep two guys happy! Give me the plebs every time for a night of fun.'

There was general laughter and romantic, not classical, music swelled sweetly into the softly illuminated darkness.

Bella pushed back her chair, jerking away Reece's hand that had found a caressing hold on her throat. She moved round the table and the hand was on her shoulder now, but she did not allow it to impede her progress.

'I'm leaving,' she exclaimed, 'right now! I'll find Vernon——'

Reece swung her round. 'What's the hurry?' He spoke with a drawl, but his grip on her shoulder told of an anger under iron control.

'I just don't like your friends,' she flared, 'your *patrician* friends. They're just that bit too up-market for my low, *plebeian* tastes.'

She tried to disentangle herself but his hold on her would not be dislodged.

'Dance with me.' It was an order, not an invitation. His arm around her waist led her from her hiding-place, placing her unceremoniously among the dancers.

'You can't force me to,' she said through her teeth.

'Can't I?' Jaw thrust belligerently, he pulled her closer. His thighs made intimate contact with hers, forcing her to follow his every intricate step.

His innate sense of rhythm communicated with hers and she found that her body was moving in perfect unison with his. Time went by, time in which Bella discovered another side to herself. There couldn't really be— could there?—a part of her that actually wanted to melt into this man, do his bidding in a way that was so much more intimate than merely dancing with him?

Her legs were none too steady as she followed his every step. She was aware of him with all her being, her nostrils inhaling the special male scent of him. Her senses began to drown in the clamouring desires his alarmingly potent sexuality was arousing in her.

'How are things with your father?' he asked, his tone soft, his smile warm and disarming.

'My dad?' she answered dreamily, her thoughts still wandering in a mysterious and enveloping mist. 'He's fine. Tired sometimes, but that's to be expected, I suppose.' Careful, a small voice inside her made itself heard, the man you're talking to is your enemy in disguise. Irresistible he might be, but he was still an enemy, she felt it in her bones. A kind of human predator, or so his sister implied.

Although surely, she argued silently, as a businessman Reece would understand if she told him just a little of the financial difficulties that Harrison's Food Fare found itself in these days? Maybe he would even offer to help with professional advice?

'If only people would pay on time,' she declared with a sigh. 'Customers mean well, but they do let their bills pile up. Then, they either "forget" them, or, when they do come to settle up, they discover they haven't got enough and ask if they could pay just a little off, and when their husband's next pay cheque comes in, or their allowance is paid next week, they really will settle the balance...' She put back her head and gazed into his warmly smiling face. 'You know how it is?'

'Oh, yes,' he answered, his brown eyes veiled, 'I know.'

'Then,' she wondered at her unguarded tongue, but the wine she had drunk seemed to be having an effect on her out of all proportion to the quantity she had actually swallowed, 'the wholesalers we get our supplies from come down on *us* for not paying the money we owe them.' She shook her head. 'It's a vicious circle. Or a "catch twenty-two", as they say nowadays.'

He did not respond, but she felt his sympathy as if it were a tangible thing. He's not so bad, is he, this brother of Jacqueline's? she informed herself with hazy satisfaction. He understands after all.

For some time their bodies matched the empathy of their minds, Bella finding herself able to anticipate and follow every rhythmic move Reece made.

'Well?' he commented softly as dance followed dance, his dark gaze looking down into her dazed eyes, her flushed face.

She moistened her lips, chiding them for trembling at the memory of his kiss beneath the parasol. 'It's—it's a beautiful evening, isn't it?' she heard herself saying, masking with the first bit of small talk that came into her head the profound feelings he had brought to life inside her.

He laughed, head back, eyes glittering. 'Oh, beautiful,' he mocked. 'The moon's shining right on cue, the view around us leaves me gasping. But the view right here is so much more to my liking.' His eyes, half closed, slid down to her breasts as they burgeoned beneath the well-fitting floral dress and flirted so wantonly with the breadth of his chest.

She looked away, refusing to read the blatant message in his gaze. 'You're a woman and I want you,' it said. He whispered her name and her glance came winging back into a headlong collision with his.

'Hey, fellas,' a loud, familiar voice cut across the magic, 'there's our sexy little shop assistant handing out one great big invitation to the master of the house. Much more, and she'll have him in bed with her. Think we ought to warn the poor guy? After all, she's already playing around with the Canford brothers...'

Bella's sleepy eyes sprang awake. They blazed into those of her partner. Tearing away from him, she pushed through the dancers and stood squarely in the path of the man who had spoken of her so derisively.

'Much more from you, Mr Haddern,' she spat, 'and I'll be suing you for defamation of character. With all these witnesses to the slander you've been throwing my way this evening, I couldn't fail to win my case.'

Malcolm jerked back, some of his drink spilling. He dabbed ineffectually at it, an unpleasant smile flowing across his face. Bella took a breath to retaliate against the implied insult she saw there, then felt herself pulled roughly round to face her partner.

'Calm down,' Reece said tersely. 'It's party-time. Let's dance.' His tone was so cool, and he appeared so unmoved by his friend's calculated innuendoes, Bella wanted to hit out as all the old enmity rekindled in her mind.

'Thanks,' she stormed, 'for standing up for me against the insults of your wonderful *friends*. Party or no party, I've had just about enough.'

He pulled her against him but she struggled. His hold would not loosen but she gritted her teeth against the pain one last tug would inflict. With it she freed herself, rubbing wherever his hands had gripped. She confronted him, head high, fists tight at her sides.

'I hate you, Mr Denman,' she got out, 'and everything that goes with you. This—this house,' it was a lie, she loved it, 'your high and mighty social circle, all—all except your sister. She's great, she stands out from the crowd, *your* crowd.'

'Hey, you two,' Jacqueline materialised beside them, 'what goes on? This is a party, for heaven's sake. What's my big brother doing to you? Get my pal Bella a drink, Dick——'

'Thanks, but no,' Bella interrupted. 'I'm not staying. It's been a lovely party, but——' Dismayed, she heard the waver, felt moisture welling behind her eyes.

'Jacqueline.' Reece's head moved, indicating, I'll deal with this. His sister shrugged and melted away.

Reece's arms went round Bella's rigid body. In spite of herself, she could not fail to feel their magic. She almost succumbed to their invitation, then remembered his indifference to his friend's slurs on her character and resisted their temptation with all her strength.

His arms dropped away, and she could not prevent a sense of profound disappointment from sweeping over her.

Then she told herself again that it was hate alone that she felt for him, not only for the inborn authority his upbringing and parents' wealth had given him, but for the almost irresistible attractiveness with which he had surely been born.

'So you hate me, hm?' His heavy-lidded eyes went on the old familiar path over her body.

'Yes, I do,' she retorted, 'and everything that you represent.' She looked around but did not care that the other guests were plainly amused by her outburst. 'I'm going home. And if I never see you again, I just won't care.'

His eyes had turned arctic, his manner remote and unapproachable. Inside, Bella trembled, but outwardly she forced herself to appear in complete control of her emotions.

'Vernon.' He had come to stand beside her. 'H-home?' She cleared her throat. She *would* keep her feelings under control. 'Please, Vernon,' she took his proffered arm, 'take me home.'

CHAPTER THREE

'YOU'RE good to us Canfords,' Jimmy said to Bella in Throttle Garage's cluttered office. 'Isn't she, Dad?'

James Canford senior nodded over the smoking bowl of his pipe. 'She certainly is. I wish you'd take some money, lass, for the work you do for us.'

Bella smiled, shaking her head. 'You can't charge friends for the help you give them. Anyway, I enjoy it. All these figures,' she pointed to the firm's cash books they had been poring over, 'they exercise my brain.'

Jimmy smiled, closing the books she had referred to. 'That's enough for *my* brain for one evening.' Hesitantly, he touched Bella's arm. 'I'll take you home.'

'Good thing Vernon's not here,' his father said with a smile, puffing on his pipe. 'You two'd be fighting over who's going to take her, probably. Which of you has got designs on her, I wonder? You, son?'

'Be quiet, Dad.'

Bella laughed and Jimmy blushed in spite of his twenty-eight years. He was, Bella had long realised, painfully shy where women were concerned, uncertain of himself and restrained even in the lightest of kisses he had given her when they had parted after the many innocent dates they had had.

He was so different from his younger brother, less outgoing than Vernon, who kissed with enthusiasm and little subtlety. And with neither brother had she felt the slightest emotion, and certainly not the leaping response of her reflexes as when Reece had kissed her the other evening at Jacqueline's party.

Even now, at the mere thought of Reece's lips on hers, those feminine reflexes of hers to her dismay started reacting. Feeling her colour rise, she moved from the desk and reached for her jacket, hurriedly pulling it on.

Jimmy pulled up outside Harrison's Food Fare. His car was more conventional than his brother's and made less noise. 'Like a coffee?' Bella asked, expecting him to refuse, but this time he agreed. She was not worried by his acceptance. Jimmy knew by experience that her invitation meant just that—coffee, a chat, a kiss on the cheek and 'Bye until next time.'

She liked the Canford brothers equally well. What their true feelings were for her she did not know. It was doubtful if they ever quarrelled over her, as she treated each of them the same—a brief kiss, followed by a promise to see them again soon.

'Sure it's OK for me to come in?' Jimmy asked, pointing out a large car that was parked just in front of his. 'Your dad got visitors?'

'No,' Bella answered with certainty. 'His friends don't own cars that size.'

Jimmy followed her along the path through the small garden that led towards the private entrance door. On the way he stopped to pick a spray of primroses and caught Bella's shoulder.

'Here,' he said awkwardly, 'got a buttonhole?'

Bella, touched by the gesture which meant so much from such a shy man, said, 'Here's one free on my blouse.'

She went to take the posy but, with a fumbling touch, Jimmy pushed it into place, the nerves in his fingers seeming to jump as they made fleeting contact with her smooth skin.

Bella smiled her thanks. 'That was a lovely thing to do, Jimmy.'

He shrugged as if it was of little consequence, but Bella knew that that was not so. 'You help us out a lot in the office,' he grunted, indicating that she should open the door, since time was too precious to be wasted in hanging around.

Bella was smiling as she entered, but the smile faded as her father's voice paused and another, only too familiar to Bella, took up the point he had made.

'Your dad *has* got company,' Jimmy said, 'so I'd better not——'

'Coffee I offered you,' Bella insisted, tight-lipped, 'and it's coffee I'll give you.'

Putting her head round the living-room door, she forced a smile. 'Hi, Dad. I'm back. Jimmy's with me.' Her face straightened as she said tonelessly, 'Good evening, Mr Strangor-Denman.' She knew that her use of his full name would annoy him, but she intended to annoy him even more. 'What are you doing visiting the Harrisons' rabbit hutch? Slumming it?'

Her father shot forward in his seat, his hands clutching the chair's arms. 'If you were ten years younger, lass, I'd send you to your room for that bit of impudence.'

'Don't let it worry you, Mr Harrison,' said Reece with a taut smile. 'Ever since I've reappeared on the Windhamleigh scene, I've been clouted left and right with insults from your daughter. I'm tough. It bounces off.'

But his eyes gave a glimpse once again of smouldering anger resolutely damped down. Then, accompanying a nod, they lifted to rest on Jimmy, lowering again to Bella. The curl of his lips added to the faint but unmistakable message of contempt his eyes held.

Like Malcolm—and how many others in the town?—he was clearly classing her as a no-good type because of her friendship with the two brothers. Well, she would show him how much she cared about his opinion, let alone the condemnation of the rest of Windhamleigh's inhabitants.

'Jimmy,' she smiled radiantly up at him, 'I promised you coffee.' She took his hand. 'Come with me. I know somewhere that we won't be interrupted.'

'Eh, but Bella...'

With a finger to her lips, she tiptoed out, drawing him conspiratorially behind her.

The door closed and she relaxed. 'It's OK,' she reassured him. 'I was only fooling. That Reece Denman, he—well, he really gets me. Right here.' She pressed her fist to her throat.

That apart, it was where he also 'got' her whenever she saw him that worried her so: her insides turning upside-down, her legs going into near meltdown—not to mention her heart's inexplicable behaviour, diving, then soaring.

'He's OK,' Jimmy said, seating himself on a stool and accepting the home-made biscuit that Bella offered him. 'Vernon said how much business he put our way the other night at that party.'

'I know.' Bella busied herself arranging cups. She knew her father would welcome a coffee, and assumed that their guest would also accept a cup if offered one. But she and Jimmy wouldn't be joining them.

Carrying the tray into the living-room, she was taken off guard by Reece's striding across to take it from her.

'Two cups?' he queried, eyebrow raised. 'Who's not having one?'

Bella steadily ignored Reece's question. 'A cup for you, Dad. Yes? And there's one for you, Mr Denman. That is, if you'll be so *condescending* as to join a member of the Harrison family——'

The threatening forward jerk of Reece's jaw stopped her flow of words, the flash of his dark eyes daring her to continue.

'Yes,' remarked Edgar reminiscently, unable because of where he sat to witness the heated, though silent interchange between his two companions, 'it's a good many years now since a member of your family joined us at the meal table, Reece. Young Jacqueline, she used to come here secretly time and again for tea when she and Bella were at school together.'

'Oh, did she?' Jacqueline's brother remarked, pretending to disapprove, but Bella was convinced that he really was annoyed at the bit of past history her father had let slip.

'Dad, Jimmy and I will be taking our coffee——' Bella shot a fighting glance in Reece's direction '—in the servants' quarters.'

She escaped along the hallway with her father's indignant reprimand ringing in her ears.

Ten minutes later, Jimmy rose to go, having tossed his coffee down as if time were baying at his heels. Bella, disappointed, wished for her own sake that he was not always so eager to get on with his life. With Jimmy gone, there would be no reason why she should not join her father and Reece, except to go to her room, which she did not fancy since it was still far too early to go to bed.

Also, an irritating voice inside her head was insisting, with Reece right here, actually on your territory, in your own home, the last thing you really want to do is to walk the other way, isn't it?

Lingering in the hallway after seeing Jimmy to his car, Bella heard her father call her name. Reluctantly she obeyed his summons. If, she pondered, I pretend that Reece isn't there . . .

'Want me to clear the empties, Dad?' she asked with a false brightness, guessing by instinct that her father had other things on his mind.

'Later, Bella, later.' His unaccustomed irritation brought her eyes swinging round to the man who, she was sure, was the cause of it.

The deliberate blankness in his eyes made her heart sink. The old familiar dissension between them was making the air sing, but its note to Bella's ears was more discordant than ever.

'What's happening?' she asked her father, fearing the answer.

'Sit down, love.' Feeling an overpowering need to do so, she obeyed. 'Tell her, Reece.'

'No, you tell me, Dad!' she could not help exclaiming. Now she was more afraid than ever, sensing that something momentous was about to break.

Jacqueline's words echoed in Bella's head. 'Strong Nation Holdings are big fish these days. They're stalking little fish...swallowing them whole...'

'I know you help me with our books, Bella,' Edgar was saying, 'but there are things I haven't told you. Like the bank ringing up the other day and warning me they couldn't give me much longer to get our sums right and——'

'Get to the point, Dad, *please*.'

'Reece,' Edgar gestured, 'he's offered to help us out. He's a good lad——'

'But, Father,' the cry was wrenched from her, 'don't you understand? You might have known Reece Denman from when he was a small boy, but he's——' her frightened eyes swung to the man she was speaking of '—he's not a "lad" now. He's a big, important man of business...his company, it's swallowing little fish whole.' At her father's puzzled frown, she added, 'That's what Jacqueline said. She warned me. I didn't believe her the other day, but I should, I should have! And I should have told you. Now he's taken you in——'

'Keep your cool, Miss Harrison.'

The even tones incensed her. She wanted to rush across and use her fists on that implacable face, his chest, wherever she could reach.

Instead, she heard herself cry, 'What do *you* know, Mr Denman, about family love and loyalty?' A flicker of pain passed across his eyes, but she didn't care, because, she told herself, she had wanted to hurt him, hadn't she? 'About loyalty to the customers of a little shop like ours? They're individuals to us. We're closer to them, care about them personally, about their problems and their troubles. We're not like those big, impersonal supermarkets you know all about. My father and I, we're good, old-fashioned traders, we've——'

'"Old-fashioned", Miss Harrison, is the word that matters. Everybody, sooner or later, has to come out of the past. And sentiment doesn't pay bills.'

'*Sentiment*? Is that how you dismiss our common touch, our plain old humanity?'

'Hush, love,' her father urged. 'Don't——'

'Don't antagonise the enemy, you're saying? Because that's what he is, Dad, make no mistake. He's a cold, calculating businessman through and through, threatening our livelihood. He's no knight in shining armour come to rescue us from...'

He is, a treacherous voice whispered, he's yours, *your* shining knight, that one special man you've been looking for all your life... See him sitting there, outwardly so relaxed, yet with lightning in his eyes and thunder in that handsome face of his. But look at his mouth, it's set and hard, that mouth that captured yours the other evening and made yours tremble and part...

'Shall I explain the proposition that's under discussion between your father and myself?' Reece asked, breaking into her reverie.

'Proposition', 'under discussion'—it all sounded so businesslike and dispassionate, she shuddered to think what might be coming.

'If you like,' she answered, pretending indifference.

'Don't be like that, Bella,' Edgar protested. 'Reece heard about our troubles and thought he might help.'

'How did he hear?' Bella asked, frowning. Then it all came back to her . . . a glass or two of wine, the seductive music, Reece's arms around her, her body bending with every little movement his had made. That fantastic smile of his had disarmed her, drawing confessions from her unguarded tongue which, in normal circumstances, she would have kept under strict control.

The telephone rang and Bella started up to answer it but her father got there first. 'Probably for me,' he said, 'about a game of chess I promised to play. Tell her, Reece, while I'm out.'

Edgar's voice rose in greeting to the caller. 'Glad to hear from you, Les.'

Bella closed the door, turning fiery eyes on Reece. 'Tell me what?' she challenged. 'As if I can't guess. You were clever, weren't you, at Jacqueline's party? You forced our secrets from me——'

'*I* was clever? I *forced* your secrets from you?' He was as angry as she was now. 'Oh, no. As I recall,' his eyes held a glacier-coldness, 'and my recollection, I know for certain, is less clouded by an over-indulgence in alcohol at the time than yours——'

'But I didn't have more than two all evening.'

He was not listening. He broke in harshly, 'It all came pouring out, didn't it, the sorry story of unpaid bills, of creditors shouting for their money? All in an effort to play on my sympathies, and get round me——' he jabbed his chest '—me, Reece "rolling-in-it" Denman, in a position of influence, plus, as you no doubt calculated when deciding to tell me your financial "sob story", a million or more of ready cash at my command.'

Bella was shaking her head, but again he ignored her protest. How could she tell him the truth—that it had all spilt out under the influence, not of alcohol, but of his attractiveness, his magnetic personality, and the way he made her feel that the words had come pouring out?

'And there you were,' he went on relentlessly, 'exploiting the situation to the full, the daughter of a small, struggling shopkeeper desperately in need of financial assistance to prevent him from descending into the abyss of bankruptcy.'

She had to defend herself! 'You encouraged me to talk, you actually *asked* me how things were with my father.'

But hadn't her inner caution tried to stop her, to remind her that this was a 'predator', an *enemy* she was confiding in? And might not his question have been merely a friendly query as to her father's health? And, instead of seeing it as such, she had plunged headlong into an explanation of their business woes and worries!

'You even let me kiss you,' he persisted, 'tolerating my lips even though you hated my guts. I was a fool, wasn't I, to miss such an opportunity? Just how much further, I wonder, would you have gone in *prostituting* yourself to gain your ends?'

'You're wrong,' she returned, stung by the underlying innuendo, every fibre of her protesting at the unjustness of his accusations, 'you're insulting me. I——' I loved you kissing me? And I shall never forget how wonderful it felt to be dancing in your arms? She could never say those words to him, and even if she did he wouldn't believe her.

Edgar's head was round the door when the phone rang again. He disappeared to answer it.

'I've offered to buy your father out,' Reece said curtly. 'To settle his bills——'

'Settle our bills? You—you really mean that? That would be wonderful. It would enable us to start again with a clean sheet. Thank you——'

'Not so fast with your gratitude,' he broke in cynically. 'We would close this shop.'

'You can't mean it?' she whispered. 'Close Harrison's Food Fare? But it's been here for years. What would our customers do?'

'Go elsewhere. There's Columbine's in the town centre.'

'But it's so big and impersonal.'

Reece shrugged. 'Strong Nation Holdings have bought it. We're rebuilding it in sections. Another two months or so and it should be ready for the official opening.'

'Bella,' Edgar appeared in the doorway. 'Mrs Edbury rang. She wants something from the shelves. She'll be round in a few minutes. I'd be glad if you'd attend to her, love.'

'It's after hours, Dad. Strictly we shouldn't serve her.'

He looked a little uncomfortably at their guest. 'It's all right, dear. She won't come in, if you can get what she wants from the shelves first, then hand it to her at the door the moment she arrives. I told her to settle tomorrow. Her little boy's not well, the doctor's been. A bottle of antiseptic is what she wants, largest size. Sorry about the interruption, Reece.' He seated himself. 'Have you told her——?' He indicated his daughter's retreating figure.

It was on the topmost shelf. It would be, Bella thought, moving the steps. Her father didn't keep that size lower down as it was not often in demand.

Climbing up, she reached high, pulling towards her the cardboard box which contained the larger bottles. The step-ladder creaked and trembled, its old wood protesting.

Bella paused, then tugged the box nearer. It was lighter in weight than she had anticipated and banged against her chest with a force that unbalanced her, pushing her backwards.

The steps wobbled and Bella's hand grasped the first thing within reach. It was the cardboard box. It went with her as she fell. As she hit the uncarpeted floor, a cry escaped her, the box glancing off her forehead and landing right side up, its contents surprisingly still in place.

Bella knew by the pain in her back and head that she was hurt more seriously than she had first thought. Her wrist, which had taken her weight as she had hit the floor, had also begun to throb.

Attempting to rise, she felt a sickening spasm in her back, sinking down again on to the floor's uncompromising hardness. A sob which she could not stifle jerked from her throat.

'Stay there, don't move.' Reece was round the counter and smoothing her brow and looking into her eyes. Don't fool yourself, she joked sadly, there's no warmth in his gaze, only a clinical assessment of your condition.

'I'm OK,' she assured him weakly. 'Give me a minute and I'll——' Again she attempted to rise, but her back cried out at the movement.

There was a ring at the door and her father, who had been crouching over her, fright in his eyes, rose hurriedly. 'Mrs Edbury. I'll go.'

'It was that box that brought me down, Dad,' Bella managed, closing her eyes as a throbbing started in her head. 'I expect the bottles are broken——'

'They're OK, love. Here, Mrs Edbury.' Edgar opened the door enough only to hand the bottle through. 'Pay tomorrow, as I said. Hope your kiddy's better soon.'

He closed the door on his customer's profuse thanks.

'Doctor,' said Reece, and put his hand lightly over Bella's mouth to silence her protests.

She experienced the most alarming impulse to press those fingers to her lips and kiss them. Instead, she turned her head so that his hand slipped away.

'I'll ring him,' Edgar offered and went back into the house.

'I can't stay here,' Bella protested, seeing for the first time from an unaccustomed angle the shop's fitments and fixtures, and noting their sorry state after years of use and neglect through an almost continuous shortage of ready cash to remedy the decay. 'I'll try to stand.' Again she attempted to rise, but without success.

'Doc Meeson said give him ten minutes,' Edgar announced, returning. 'And not to move her.'

Reece looked around and discovered a pile of old newspapers, easing them under Bella's head. 'Not goose down, nor even feathers,' he remarked with a faint smile, 'but better than nothing, hm?'

Bella smiled her thanks. He wandered round and she watched him apprehensively. What would those keen eyes of his discover? He paused now and then, studying the shelves, peering into the chilled display cabinets and opening doors. She grew agitated, wishing he wouldn't, knowing that many things other than the fitments had been somewhat neglected over the years.

The doctor arrived, examining Bella, asking questions, testing and pressing. 'Bruised,' was his verdict, 'in slight shock too, judging by her paleness, but no concussion, nor bones broken. Your back will dictate to what extent you'll be able to move, Bella. You must go carefully for a while,' he advised, 'then a gentle return to work. Reece?' He knew the Strangor-Denman family as well as he knew the Harrisons. 'Would you do a kindly deed and carry this wounded heroine to wherever she wants to go? But take great care with her back, won't you?' The doctor left with a lift of the hand.

Reece stared down at her, hands on hips, his expression enigmatic. Then he broke into a smile.

'It depends,' he said, 'whether the lady in question wants me to help her. Normally, she tolerates me only with very bad grace. Would you prefer it, Miss Harrison,' he quipped, 'if your father were to ring for one of the Canford brothers to carry you wherever you want to go?'

'I don't know what you mean,' Bella returned spiritedly. 'What's so special about Vernon and Jimmy that you think I might prefer them to——' careful, she reproached herself, you so nearly gave yourself away! '——to anyone else?' she finished airily.

'Right,' said Reece, in a rolling-up-his-sleeves tone, crouching beside Bella, 'if I do this,' he slid his hands under her, 'and this,' slowly, gently, he began to lift her, 'does it hurt?'

'Just——' She gritted her teeth. 'Just a little. But d-don't let it stop you.' She couldn't tell him, The mere fact that I'm in your arms is acting like an analgesic. 'Anything to lie on something soft and——' 'Clean', she had so nearly said, and what would have been more calculated to make him look around for the blemishes that she had spied? 'Comforting,' she added.

'For God's sake tell me,' Reece said, carefully hoisting her higher, 'if you can't stand being carried.'

'Don't worry, I will.' Her head flopped against his shoulder, his sweet breath fanned her face, his thick, daunting eyebrows were near enough to trace—if her finger had had the right. Which it hadn't, she told herself sharply, and never would.

Reece carried her to her bedroom, lowering her so that she lay flat as the doctor had recommended. He stared down at her, expression thoughtful, fingers slipped into his waistband. 'Now what?' he asked.

She managed a smile. 'A typically masculine reaction.'

'And you, of course, know the A to Z of masculine reactions. I thought as much. With *two* boyfriends to play around with——'

'Stop it!' Bella cried, half lifting herself in her annoyance. 'Stop talking like your wonderful friend Malcolm Haddern.' She groaned at the pain the movement had inflicted and dropped back. 'For your information, I wasn't out with Jimmy on a date this evening. I was helping him and his father with their office work. Anyway,' she stared belligerently up at him, 'why should I explain my actions to you? I can go out with—*and stay in with*—whoever I like.'

It seemed by his expression that she had achieved the reaction she had intended. Hadn't she used those provocative words simply to annoy him?

'So,' he commented cynically, 'the rumours about your liking for male company in the plural aren't far wrong. I should have known. No smoke, they say, without conflagration.'

'My moral code is my affair, Mr Denman, not yours, nor anybody else's.' She half rose again, but the recoil in her back was so painful a cry escaped her, and tears brimmed. They were not, she was well aware, caused only by her injured spine, but by Reece's cynical condemnation of her friendship with the two Canford brothers.

'OK, OK,' he soothed, without an atom of sympathy, 'keep calm. Your life's *your* life. And you're a big girl now.' Male eyes traced the slender shape of her as she lay prone, lingering on her hips, the swell of her breasts, and, as if he could hardly contain his impulse to meet them with his own, her full, inviting lips.

She tried in vain to halt the tide of colour that crept into her cheeks, and his smile taunted her in her discomfiture. He too had known what her reaction would be to his words and, like her, had no doubt deliberately drawn it from her.

He extracted a tissue from the box at her bedside and, with a series of near caresses, dried the tears that had escaped to trickle down her cheeks.

'Thank you for your help,' Bella said, attempting to still the action of his hand. The tenderness of his touch was almost too much to bear, despite the throb of her injuries. She managed to grip his arm, feeling the dark hairs spring tantalisingly beneath her palms. 'You—you can go now.'

Then she realised she had used her injured hand and winced, letting go. He took the hand, inspecting the painful wrist and lifting it slowly to his lips. These he rested on it, his eyes holding hers. In a panic at the excitement the intimate touch of his mouth was arousing, she tried to remove her hand, but could not for pain.

'Got you,' he murmured, his gaze bright with victory, then he replaced her hand on the bed covers. 'What are we going to do with you?' he queried. 'You can't just lie there like that. Who's going to help you undress, wash, get into bed?'

'Bella?' came Edgar's voice from downstairs. 'Is Reece with you?'

'Yes, Dad, but he's on his way.'

'Tell him I'd like a word before he leaves.'

'Will do, Mr Harrison.' Reece turned back to Bella. 'Want me to contact Jacqueline? She'd gladly come over and give you a hand.'

'Nobody, thank you,' was her firm answer as she turned her face away. 'Dad will come if I need help.'

'Here.' Reece's hand pushed into his pocket and Bella opened her eyes. Jimmy's posy of flowers perched precariously on her chest. 'I picked them up when I lifted you. I thought you wouldn't want your boyfriend's touching love token to die neglected on the cold shop floor.'

She heard the false sentiment and flashed him a quelling look. Unquelled, he smiled in response.

She held the flowers carefully. 'It was a nice gesture on Jimmy's part, nothing else. But, knowing you, I wouldn't expect you to believe that.'

'You *know* me back to front, do you?' he grated.

'I've known *of* you for a good many years now, Mr Strangor-Denman. And,' she knew her words would goad him but she didn't care, 'I doubt if anyone, *any woman*, could ever know the enigmatic, chauvinistic Reece *Strangor*-Denman back to front.'

'If you've known *of* me for so long, *Miss Harrison*,' he thundered back, 'then you should also know that I have long since dropped the "Strangor" part of my name. So will you quit using it as a term of abuse?' He had spoken so angrily, Bella's conscience jolted her, and she felt she should try to make amends at least to the extent of thanking him again for his help. This she did.

He acknowledged her words with a nod that had no warmth about it, then left her without another word. For a long time afterwards, she heard his voice, muffled and low, as he talked to her father. She fell asleep wondering just what kind of decisions they were making while she, the awkward one, was safely out of the way.

CHAPTER FOUR

NEXT morning Bella discovered the answer. It presented itself in the form of a middle-aged lady appearing at her bedside, having first asked permission.

'Your father would have introduced me, dear,' the smiling, plump and neatly dressed visitor announced, 'if he hadn't been so busy with the customers. So I shall have to introduce myself. I'm Maddy Langridge. I lost my husband a few years ago. You might have seen me around the town in the distant past?'

Bella, puzzled, shook her head.

'No? Well, I don't actually live here, but in a village a few miles away. You see, I used to be the Strangor-Denman children's nanny.'

Bella frowned. 'You must have been very young at the time.'

Maddy laughed and thanked Bella for the compliment.

'Thanks for calling, Mrs Langridge, but . . .' Then the penny dropped. 'Mr Strangor-Denman has asked you to come and look after me? Really, there's no need——'

Maddy laughed again. 'He warned me you would say that, Miss Harrison.'

'Please call me Bella.'

'Well, that's a step in the right direction. One hurdle crossed, as they say. Please call me Maddy, short for Madeleine. Reece and Jacqueline always did. By the way, I'm a semi-retired nurse.' She looked around. 'Let me get my bearings, and then I can judge what's needed.'

'Oh, but Mrs—I mean, Maddy——' My father isn't in a position to pay for a nurse, she had been about to say, when Mrs Langridge broke in.

'If it's payment for my services you're worried about, then forget it, dear. Mr Denman—as he likes to be called—is taking care of that side.'

'No, he can't. That's not right. He——'

Mrs Langridge laughed again. 'He told me you would say that, too. Don't worry, Bella. He's very comfortably off. He always was clever, even as a little boy. I knew he would have a brilliant future. Now,' she raised a cautioning hand, 'no more protests. I'm here to look after you.'

And this she proceeded to do for some days, returning every morning, until Bella had recovered sufficiently to walk around, look after herself and eventually descend the stairs.

Bella liked Maddy Langridge, but was so concerned that the cost of that lady's services was coming out of Reece's pocket that she made up her mind to get back to normal as fast as her injuries would allow.

One evening after Maddy had left, Bella half lay on the living-room sofa. She and her father had had their evening meal, prepared by Maddy before she left. Now, Bella was alone for the first time since her fall. Edgar had gone to a meeting of the chess club.

'Sure you'll be all right?' he had asked, pulling on his jacket. 'I don't like going off and leaving you like this. Pity Vernon and Jimmy were both working flat out at the garage when I rang them and couldn't come and keep you company.'

'I'll be fine,' she had assured him again.

He'd smiled, patted her head and said he wouldn't be late.

Wrapped as she was in the sounds coming from the headphones of her personal radio, she did not hear the door to the private entrance open and close. When a tall, masculine figure loomed over her as she lay lost in the music, her eyes sprang open and her heart almost jumped from her chest.

With shaky hands she removed the headphones and stared into Reece's sardonic gaze. 'You gave me a terrible fright,' she accused. 'How did you get in? Dad always shuts the door securely behind him.'

'I was at Throttle Garage when he rang through to the Canfords. I called in on the chess meeting and got this from him.' He held up the key. 'He said he had a duplicate tucked away, and to leave this here when I left.'

'Why have you come?' Bella asked belligerently. 'I told Dad I didn't need company, so——' emphasising her meaning by staring at the door '—thanks for coming.'

He didn't stir. Instead he looked down at her with a mixture of amusement that enraged and a muted exasperation that pleased her.

He answered at last, 'I heard the Canford brothers give a regretful "no" to your father's request and, softhearted guy that I am,' his smile was both cynical and provoking, 'I couldn't bear the thought of helpless little Isabella Harrison lying here all alone.'

'Oh, yes?' Bella answered disbelievingly. 'The Reece Denman I know,' she added, 'is anything but softhearted.'

A quizzical eyebrow lifted but he didn't respond. Looking idly round, he jangled the change in his pocket, then picked up the headphones which Bella had forgotten to switch off. For a few minutes he listened, tapping his foot, his eyes resting on her contemplatively.

Bella shifted uncomfortably under his scrutiny, absentminded though it seemed to be. He plainly recognised her discomfiture and smiled enigmatically. Removing the headphones, he bent to switch off the radio and wandered round the room.

With a jolt, Bella remembered the way he had roamed around the shop as they had waited for the doctor. Now, she looked with Reece's eyes at the place she and her parents had lived in for so long.

She saw the shabbiness, the worn patches, the deteriorating decorations. There had never seemed to be quite enough money to spare to refurbish and renew. Her heart sank at what she saw, and she felt the need to justify and defend.

'Jacqueline used to love coming here in the old days,' she heard herself say.

He turned slowly and came to stand beside the sofa, eyebrows raised. 'So?'

'Well,' she shrugged, looking anywhere but at him, 'there's no need to be so critical about the way my dad and I live.'

'For God's sake, have I said a word?'

'No, but...' Her stare bounced off him and on to their surroundings. 'I can sense the criticism, I can *feel* what you're thinking.'

'What have we here?' he asked cuttingly. 'An expert mind-reader? You know exactly what your customers are going to ask for before they speak?'

She turned her face away. 'Don't be silly.'

He walked off again, trying out a musical box for sound, inspecting the books on a series of shelves.

'Reece?' she asked, her voice sounding loud in the silence. He did not turn, but she guessed by the way he grew still that he was listening. 'Please leave Harrison's Food Fare alone. The customers will pay their bills eventually. They always do. Well, apart from the odd one or two.'

This time he faced her, remaining where he was. 'You can stop fighting that particular battle. I settled the matter with your father the other evening. I withdrew my offer.'

Her heart jumped, then dived. But why, she asked herself, when she should be glad? She should be clapping her hands, doing a cartwheel if her back had let her. Did it mean that on the evening of her fall he had spied the degenerating state of the premises as she had feared he might?

'The idea of my buying your father out has been dropped,' he went on, tucking his shirt more securely into his waistband, an action which seemed to Bella to be curiously personal, drawing her eyes to his lean waist, his flat stomach, the taut fit of his jeans. 'We discussed the matter in all its aspects, and came to the mutual decision that a buy-out was a non-starter. Also, your considerate father couldn't bring himself to go ahead in the face of his dear daughter's emphatic opposition.'

'Don't you mean ''stubborn and obstinate''?'

'Your words, Bella. Whatever,' with a shrug, 'put it out of your mind.'

'So, as far as Strong Nation Holdings is concerned, Harrison's Food Fare can sink or swim?'

'Look, you can't have it both ways. Either you agree to my proposition or you don't.' She shook her head. 'You don't. So stop making provocative remarks.' He looked down at her, eyes hooded. 'You threw my coat back at me when it rained. You stood me up in the middle of a dance at Jacqueline's party. You've just thrown my offer of financial help back in my face. There's a limit to what a man—let alone a businessman—can stand.'

For some reason she had to go on fighting this man who was her enemy, even though her other self was saying, Enough is enough, for heaven's sake be quiet. 'You keep a list of my social and personal misdemeanours, so as to fling them at me when I'm down?'

His anger at her words seemed to her to be excessive. '*Fling* them at you? When you're——' his eyes raked her recumbent form, then took up the fight in her belligerent eyes '—*down*? When, prostrate though you are, you're *still* attacking me verbally, like a punch-drunk boxer?' A muscle worked in his cheek, his teeth snapped together and he ground out, 'I warned you there was a limit. You goad me beyond it, so I respond. Like this.'

As he bent down, his arms insinuated themselves beneath her body, swinging her up. Then he lowered her, threading her through his hands to stand her on the floor.

'Please, my back!' she cried, but his ears were deaf to her appeal.

His arms went round her, supporting her figure, yet at the same time impelling her to him. His mouth chased hers as it dodged and evaded, fastening on her mutinous lips at last, prising them open and drinking his fill from the very depths of her.

His hand invaded her T-shirt from below, pushing upwards and skimming across her uncovered breasts, stroking one and then the other, taking captive with audacious fingertips the pouting nipples. Her legs almost gave way under the tumult of sensations he was arousing, the desire that ran amok all over her. She knew that if he didn't soon call off the chase she would be unable to stop herself from responding to his almost irresistible onslaught.

He meant it as a punishment, she knew that, but the woman in her loved what he was doing to her, she loved the feel of his arousal against the throbbing sensitivity of her inner thighs...*she loved him*! Beyond belief, she loved him. All these years she had loved him, even when he'd looked at her years ago in that certain way. He had been out of her reach then and, she told herself, he was even more beyond it now.

No, she didn't love him, she cried inside, feeling her mouth throbbing under his, shivering as his hands reached down beyond her waistband, she hated him! Just as she used to do all those years ago. He was still arrogant and imperious and autocratic. The years hadn't altered that.

This kiss he was compelling her to accept—would it never end and would his hands which were arousing her to fever pitch never stop their erotic roaming?—meant nothing to him except as a means of wreaking vengeance and a way of working out his anger with her for her constant verbal pinpricks. So why should it mean anything to her? Slowly he released her, his eyes blazing into hers, the anger still smouldering within him. I don't love him, she told herself fiercely, it was only under the influence of his kiss that I thought I did.

He scooped her up and with only the merest touch of gentleness returned her to the sofa, lifting her legs back on to it. As he straightened the phone rang. He looked at it, looked at her. The instrument was out of her reach.

He lifted the receiver and barked 'Yes?' He listened and passed it to her. 'One of your two *body* guards,' he cracked. 'The younger.'

Hearing Vernon's question, Bella thought, Now's my chance to prove to Reece Denman that he means nothing to me.

'Oh, Vernon,' she exclaimed, 'I'm so glad you can come round after all! It'll be a pleasure to see you if only for half an hour. No, it wasn't my dad who answered. He's still out. It was—it was someone from the privileged end of the town. Playing——' Dared she say it?

Reece was looking at her as if he would like to tear her to pieces. All the same, she added, 'Playing the patronising visitor come to enquire the state of health of one of society's lower orders who lives above the shop.'

Reece, who had swung away to stare down into the street, went quietly to the door. His restrained response to her provocation rebuked her far more than a show of anger would have done.

As his car engine burst into life, Bella's conscience reproached her forcefully. He had been so good to her since her accident. Hadn't he sent her Maddy Langridge, and hadn't he been paying that lady's salary? And for this she had given him not a single word of thanks...

'Did you hear that Columbine's is going to have an official opening?' Vernon queried one evening as he cleaned his grease-stained hands on a cloth. 'Quite soon now, they say.'

Bella had a date with him and, having arrived at the repair depot early, had been watching patiently while he put the finishing touches to an engine adjustment.

'I did overhear some of our customers talking about it,' she admitted. 'They said a big name's coming to do the honours, someone Mr Hunter-Parkes' daughter knows.'

'Yeah,' said Vernon. 'Hamish Harlequin, star of stage and screen. Harlequin...Columbine's,' he laughed wryly, 'any fool could follow the publicity guys' train of thought. Isn't Mr Hunter-Parkes' daughter Reece Denman's fancy woman?' Vernon queried after a pause, throwing aside the blackened rag.

Bella's heart tripped and steadied. Like Vernon, she had heard that piece of innuendo from the lady's father's own lips. 'He knows her well,' he had said at Jacqueline's party, adding with a wink, 'if you get my meaning.' Which, like herself, Vernon obviously had.

So what, she thought, if Reece has kissed me? Twice. Just what did that signify? The first time, he had been in a party mood, which meant that the kiss had been quite meaningless. The second time, he had intended to only humiliate and chasten. And hadn't he succeeded!

It was only natural, she told herself bluntly, that a man as dynamic and virile as Reece would have a woman in his life. More than one probably, but then Marguerite Hunter-Parkes lived in the kind of world where women's attitudes to such things were easygoing and tolerant.

All the same, Bella reflected, it didn't make it any easier for her to accept such a situation, born and bred as she had been into a close-kint and loving family environment.

Almost two months had passed since her passionate exchange with Reece. Her father had continued to go about his business in his usual competent and dedicated way, with not a mention of Reece's name, but Bella had detected a subtle change.

Maybe it was the number of times she'd caught him rubbing his eyes. With increasing frequency he spent his evenings sitting with a worried frown over the accounts or the order books. When she had asked if there was something she could do to help, he would shake his head and tell her gently that it was his business to worry, not hers.

'Who owns this sleek piece of equipment?' she asked Vernon smilingly, indicating the dark red sports car he had been working on.

'The lady we've been talking about,' Vernon answered. 'Miss Hunter-Parkes. She brought it in one day when Jimmy was here and he was so tongue-tied he could hardly get a word out. But it didn't matter,' Vernon laughed, polishing the red exterior with a vigour that made it shine, 'because the lady customer talked so much all he had to do was listen! But has she got fantastic——' with his hands he sketched a female shape '—bodywork. Not her car,' he added with a grin.

Bella smiled too, thinking sarcastically, Great for Mr Strangor-Denman! Tired of merely standing around, she took up a soft cloth and followed Vernon around the vehicle, polishing the shine he had produced until it dazzled.

When a car drew up in the garage forecourt, she did not stop, being too absorbed in her self-imposed task. When car doors slammed and the occupants' shapes became reflected in the polished panels, Bella found that her arm was rubbing frenziedly all over the reflection of the car's lady owner.

Was it, Bella wondered with wry amusement, trying its best, on her behalf, to rub that lady away from the side of the man with whom she was so gracefully approaching?

That man's reflection, Bella noted with some surprise and not a little trepidation, detached itself from its female companion and came to a halt beside her own reflected image.

'Bella,' said the male reflection.

'Good evening, Mr Denman,' was her precise and formal answer. Don't look at him, she told herself, just carry on working. While the other two discussed the car's mechanical troubles, which Vernon and his brother had so competently fixed, Bella carried on polishing, the only evidence of her agitation being in the way her hand moved in even faster circles.

'Working here part time?' the maddening male reflection silkily enquired. 'Earning yourself some extra pocket money?' She did not respond. 'Shop sales fallen that low, then?'

'No!' shot from her too hastily, her head jerking up, as the questioner had known it would. His solid substance, she discovered, was in even better shape to issue cynical taunts than the glossy shadow of him had been.

Those mocking eyes glinted. 'Giving a helping hand for free?' He glanced across at Vernon who was still deep in conversation with Marguerite Hunter-Parkes. 'Or for love?'

'I'm doing it,' Bella retorted, 'because I'm——' The cloth fell from her fingers and Bella bent to snatch it from the dirt and dust. Why, she thought, shaking it out, should she explain to this arrogant male? 'Because I'm doing it,' she finished tartly, and returned to her task.

Marguerite, her attention having been attracted by Bella's snapping tone, strolled across to Reece's side.

'What goes on?' she enquired languidly, her almond-shaped eyes flashing messages which only Reece could interpret.

'Insubordination among the lower orders,' Reece replied, watching Bella.

Bella's intake of breath was sharp, the riposte ready on her lips when she saw his mockery. Then she recalled her own use of the expression the last time she had seen him when he had called on her in her father's absence.

'I——' she began, carrying on with her self-imposed task, then stared, horrified, at the car's bodywork. A long black line flaunted itself over the shiny surface. Oh, God, she thought, what have I done?

Marguerite's eagle eye followed Bella's. She gasped and shrieked, 'Mr Canford, your assistant has damaged my car. Since you employ her, I hold you entirely responsible.' Her hands found her slender hips, her upper feminine statistics expanding and contracting at an alarming rate. 'I shall expect you to remedy the damage she's caused and, Mr Canford, if you dare to send me in a bill for *any* of the work you've done, I'll not only take away my business, but persuade my father to do so, too.'

'She's a friend, not an employee,' Vernon corrected worriedly, adding, 'Bella, love, what's happened?'

'Oh, Vernon,' Bella moaned, 'I really am sorry. When I dropped the cloth, it must have picked up some grit, although I shook it out.' It was Reece's fault really, she thought, confusing me by standing so near. She stared helplessly at the mark. 'What can I do to——?'

As she gazed, the reflection of a male arm extended and, clothed in an impeccably cut dark sleeve though it was, took possession of the offending cloth, shook it vigorously and applied it gently to the black line.

As if that arm had possessed a magic power, the line started to disappear. 'More grease solvent, Vernon,' the owner of the arm demanded crisply, and, on receiving it, proceeded to eliminate completely the cause of the discord.

Bella's hands flew to her burning face. 'R-Reece,' she stammered, 'how can I——?'

'She calls you Reece?' Marguerite demanded with asperity.

Reece ignored the question, which answered itself, really, Bella thought.

'If it's in line,' he drawled, 'with your usual method of thanking me, Miss Harrison, don't even try. I'm not in the mood for having a can of grease solvent thrown in my face.'

In a cynical twist, he had turned the tables on her and thrown her own thanks back at her. Well, she wasn't going to have ingratitude added to her list of faults, so she seized her chance to correct an omission that had been on her conscience since he had last exited from her particular scene.

'The lady you employed to look after me,' she got in just as he turned away, 'Maddy Langridge, I mean, doesn't come any more. But I expect you know that, because your bank account isn't being drained by the weekly payment of her wages.' Seeing his eyebrows rise in aloof query, she realised that the way she had framed the statement would probably have had a distinctly sarcastic sound.

Even when she was expressing her thanks, she realised, her old antipathies broke through. Would they never leave her? In a more gracious tone, she added, 'I'm much better now, as you can see.'

Reece's cool glance inspected her from top to toe, then he appeared to lose interest, but Bella persisted, 'I haven't thanked you yet for sending her. I'm thanking you now. On my father's behalf as well as my own.'

'Don't overdo the gratitude,' he replied astringently, then turned his attention entirely to the woman who plainly mattered much more to him than Bella Harrison ever would.

Waving to Vernon as he drove away, Bella let herself into the entrance hall, hearing her father's favourite music playing softly.

She listened for voices, one in particular, since she sensed the presence of a visitor, but it seemed she was wrong.

Her father was alone, reclining, head back, legs outstretched, in his chair. He seemed to be sleeping, so Bella turned to go, but he stirred, sitting up.

'Come in, lass. Turn that off, will you?' Bella did so, about to say 'I don't mind listening, too,' but noticed her father's slightly nervous movements. 'I wasn't asleep, just thinking.'

Out of the blue, Bella felt acutely apprehensive. Was her father ill, and had kept the fact hidden from her until now? Edgar read his daughter's face and smiled. 'Don't fret, dear. Nothing's wrong with me. But I'd like to talk.'

The business, she thought, placing her bag on a chair and fluffing her hair from around the collar of her dress, that's what's wrong.

Edgar commented, watching her, 'When you do that, you look so like your dear mother.' A sad, reminiscent frown came and went, then a look of concentration as the subject on his mind took over. 'Reece called to see me. Don't look so startled, lass. He didn't come to suggest a buy-out again.'

I knew it! Bella thought. I could *feel* that he'd been here.

'But,' she said aloud, 'he was at Throttle Garage with his lady-friend, Miss Hunter-Parkes, when she went to collect her car they were repairing. I'm sure he spent the evening with her.'

'Well,' Edgar laughed, 'either there's two of him or he's clever enough to be in two places at once. He certainly didn't bring that lady here. He spent nearly a couple of hours with me.'

Bella, still surprised, told herself how lucky she had been to miss their visitor, then reproached her other self for contradicting her. But it leapt at the thought that, soon afterwards, he must have ditched Marguerite, probably against her will, judging by the way she had flung her arms around his neck after he had removed the offending blemish from her car door.

'Reece Denman never calls on this place unless it's on business,' Bella offered into the stiff silence. Clearly her father was uneasy. 'So...?' she encouraged.

Her father began to speak, hesitated and was silent. Bella felt apprehension build, giving way to downright worry. Edgar gave a sigh, settled back and rubbed his forehead, a gesture Bella had, in her father, come to associate over the years with acute anxiety.

'His proposition——'

'Not another!' Bella exclaimed, now fearing the worst. 'He's going to close the shop, after all. After buying us out, I mean.'

'It's not that, dear. I told you. It's... Well, Bella,' he sat forward, 'I'll be frank. I've been feeling tired lately, bone-weary here,' he indicated his legs, 'and here,' pointing to his head. 'Both the physical effort of running this place, and all the paperwork involved, not to mention worrying about money, or rather lack of it.'

'Dad,' Bella reproached, 'you could have told me. I'd have taken more off your shoulders, spoken to the wholesalers, got the customers to produce the cash they owed.'

Her father was shaking his head. 'You're only young once, lass. I didn't want to spoil the fun you were getting out of life by weighing you down with my problems.'

'But you must have told Reece Denman,' Bella protested. 'You trusted him more than me.'

'That I did not, young lady. He's been in once or twice, bought things. It must have been when you weren't here. I suppose he used his eyes, took a guess about how I felt.'

'So,' Bella hardened herself to the answer, 'what kind of proposition is it this time?'

Edgar plainly decided he must take the plunge, and answer his daughter's question.

'Seems he's noticed I know about wines, spirits, the alcohol we sell.' He paused, as if steeling himself to go on. 'He told me that Columbine's—you know it's been extended by Strong Nation Holdings and brought right up to date? Well, they need a man to take charge of wines and spirits—that section's been enlarged, too.' A short silence, as if he himself couldn't believe his own good fortune. 'He offered me the job, Bella, and at a salary I can hardly refuse.'

Edgar stole a glance at his daughter, saw her drained cheeks and shook his head resignedly.

'I told him I didn't think you'd want me to accept, but promised to put it to you. I'll turn it down, lass, don't you worry.'

'You'll do nothing of the sort, Dad.' Her father would never know what it cost her to utter those words. 'It would be wonderful to see you doing exactly what you wanted. I know how you love that line. You've made a study, you know so much.'

'You don't seem to understand, Bella. This shop—without me here, it would have to be closed. And you'd be out of a job.'

The reality of the situation hit her so hard the world began to spin. It took only a few seconds for her mind to steady it and stop it in its tracks.

'No, I wouldn't!' she exclaimed. 'I'd take the business over and run it myself.'

CHAPTER FIVE

JIMMY joined Bella on her walk a few evenings later, taking his red setter Pansi with them, keeping the dog on a lead until they reached the open fields.

Although this was Bella's favourite path, she had not been that way since the evening she had accidentally met Reece there.

On the hilltop, Bella sat on Jimmy's jacket and stared around, hugging her knees while he, seated beside her, kept an eye on Pansi as she joyfully roamed free.

The valley cupped the town, sheltering it lovingly from the worst of any storms or gales that threatened to come its way. Stone cottages from centuries past continued undisturbed by the passage of time to nudge each other, while on the other side of the town stood the larger residences of the better off in the community.

'As a child,' Bella reminisced, gazing across, 'I thought of the people who lived over there as "them", not "us". You, too?'

Jimmy nodded, chewing a stalk of grass and looking round for his dog. 'Oh, no!' he exclaimed. 'She's missing. There she is! Pansi, here,' he yelled, but Pansi was otherwise engaged. Jimmy called again and she made a dash, her owner pounding after her, calling over his shoulder, 'Sorry, Bella, can't leave her. She's in that certain condition... Can you get yourself home?'

Bella cupped her hands and shouted that she could, then bent to rescue some flowers that Jimmy had given her, binding them with a blade of grass and inhaling their freshness.

Trying to avoid crushing underfoot the wild meadow flowers that grew in abundance all around, she contemplated without much pleasure the coming week, when her father began his new job at Columbine's. Deep in thought as she was, she did not hear the footsteps until they paced beside her.

Her heart leapt at the sight of the man to whom they belonged and she dropped the miniature bouquet. He stooped to retrieve it, handing it back.

'Hallmark of Jimmy Canford. Correct?' Reece queried, quizzical eyebrow raised.

'What if it is?' she retorted.

He affected to look around. 'Not a sign. He couldn't take "no" and left you stranded?'

'So what if he did? No, no! I mean... Oh, read what you like into my friendship with Jimmy.' She turned away.

'And Vernon?'

She swung back. 'Yes,' with defiance and an angry frown, 'and Vernon. Anyway, it wasn't like that at all. Jimmy's dog ran off and he had to go after her.'

'OK, I get the picture. So I'll walk you home.'

'No, thanks. I enjoy my own company, didn't you know?'

'Is that why you've decided to carry on alone at Harrison's?'

'If you're being funny——' she fired at him.

'Not really. Well, is it?'

'That's my business.' Her tiny bouquet was disintegrating in her moist hold. Her head lifted belligerently. 'You hoped I'd give in, didn't you? You thought that in offering Dad that plum of a job at Columbine's, plus the offer of a flat, you'd force Harrison's to close, and me out of a job. Then, you probably reasoned—in league with Strong Nation's accountants, of course—that any offer you made for the shop, not to mention the piece of land around it, would be irresistible to my father and me.'

'Did I?' His voice was cold now, his eyes at zero temperature.

'Well, you were wrong, Mr Denman. There's no way— *no way, I tell you*—you're going to close down the business that took my parents years to build up. I'll keep it going even if it kills me!'

To her horror, she burst into tears, dropping the flowers and covering her face, sinking down to the soft turf at Reece's feet and sobbing as if she would never stop. It had all come descending, like a ton weight, on to her shoulders, crushing her tired mind. She had told no one, not even her father, how many hours lately she had lain awake, worrying about the business she had been determined to run single-handed.

Arms with a strength that would not be denied lifted her, holding her against a wall of a chest which vibrated with a pounding heart. When Bella discovered she was dampening his shirt, she tried to draw away, but a soft white square was pushed between her cheek and that item of clothing and she used it, drying her tears and clutching it like a child would a precious toy.

'Go for your walk, will you?' she muttered, drawing away from him and pushing at her hair. 'I'm OK.'

'Bella,' he lifted her chin, 'my intentions towards Harrison's Food Fare have always been strictly honourable. I haven't set out since my return to do you and your father down, nor to reduce the business he's so painstakingly built up over the years to mere rubble.'

'So what has been your intention?' she challenged. 'Simply to make Columbine's so irresistible to the shopping public they leave Harrison's one by one? What's that, if not reducing it to dust? Or at least, an empty shell?'

'No doubt you'll spring at me if I utter the cliché, "That's life"?'

'You mean it's commerce, it's big business, it's dog eats dog. Well, I want none of it. I'm sure of my customers. They won't leave Harrison's. It provides them with something special, something precious that you won't find these days even in Columbine's, even in the biggest and most prestigious of stores. I'm talking about personal attention and service, by people *who care*.'

She swung away and made for home. He caught her up.

'I'll walk you.' He had caught her arm, but she tugged at his hold. 'I insist,' he added with a quiet authority with which she dared not argue.

The sun had set, leaving its glorious colours strewn across the sky. In a move to prevent any attempt she might make to break away, he had encircled her waist with his arm, his hand on her hip like a clamp. His touch made her grit her teeth, not in hatred of it but against the wanton sensations it aroused in her.

Passers-by who knew them both smiled and nodded, a hidden question in their eyes. At the side gate, Reece drew her roughly to a halt and swung her round.

'You can't, Isabella,' he said, and Bella's heart leapt at the way he said her name, 'escape the inevitable. Face up to it, and life will become a darned sight easier for you all round.'

His gaze dropped to her lips, appeared to consider, then seemed to change its mind. He released her and she tossed back her wind-blown hair, fighting a treacherous sense of disappointment.

'Thanks for bringing me home, Mr Denman,' she said. 'As for the "inevitable" you mentioned, I don't accept that it is, so I don't have to face up to it, do I?'

'If you ever need help——'

'Thank you again,' was her defiant answer, 'but you'd be the last person I'd turn to. The sort of help I might need, and I hope I never do, wouldn't be the kind you would offer. I'm only going by past experience of your offers of "help" to my father and me.'

He swung on his heel and strode away.

Bella attended the opening ceremony of the enlarged and redesigned Columbine's. She had left her new assistant, Polly Meeson, in charge.

Reece, she reflected, was certain to be there so, not wanting to be recognised, either by him or by her father, whom she had not told of her intention, she wore a pair of 'play' spectacle frames which Polly had discovered among the shop's stock, and piled her hair high, securing it with slides. From her ears dangled long and heavy earrings which one of her aunts had sent her in her teens. She had been liberal with the make-up, too, and wore a two decades old two-piece suit of her mother's which had somehow escaped being given to charity.

She found a place among the crowd. The store was packed to its doors and beyond. As she watched the proceedings, her heart slipped a notch with each round of applause from the plainly impressed spectators. They, it seemed, could hardly wait for the proceedings to end before descending on the display cabinets and multiplicity of shelves and allow their money to flow out of their purses and pockets and into the coffers of the mighty Strong Nation Holdings.

Reece looked debonair and incredibly handsome in his finely cut suit and the ladies around Bella commented on his appearance.

'I'd have thought,' said one, 'that he—him, Mr...' she consulted the 'programme' each person had been given '...Reece Denman, that *he'd* be the film star. He's better looking than Hamish Harlequin.'

'I think he's gorgeous,' declared another, 'Mr Denman, I mean. He belongs to Windhamleigh, did you know? Born and bred here.' She nudged her neighbour. 'Wish my husband had his looks. He was born and bred here, too!'

Reece introduced his members of staff, ending, Bella saw, watching with a daughterly love and pride, with her father. He also had dressed in his best although it was, as Bella knew, well-worn, but it was the only suit he currently possessed.

As the opening ceremony ended, the people around her dispersed with such speed all over the store that she was left standing alone, feeling over-warm and irresolute about her next move. She longed to make contact with her father, but Reece was still hovering and she dared not cross to that area of the store.

Looking around, she felt herself drawn to the displays, recognising the artifice with which they had been arranged in order to tempt the customers to buy and buy again, filling their trolleys and baskets.

There was something missing, she told herself, and it *wasn't* sour grapes, nor envy, she silently defended herself to the commanding, if distant figure of Reece Denman. People, she noticed, members of staff probably, approached him almost deferentially. When she remembered the way she had spoken to him sometimes, she blushed beneath her disguise.

Her father gazed around almost as if he had felt her presence, so she dodged behind a pillar until his attention was distracted by a customer. Finding a group of chatting customers to weave her way through, she sighed with relief as she made it unrecognised through the exit doors.

Making for her room, Bella hurriedly divested herself of her disguise, pulling on the white blouse and dark skirt which she always wore when serving in the shop.

Catching her as she entered through the rear office, Polly Meeson whispered, 'Glad you're back. Could you come, Bella? There's a man wandering round looking at the shelves and things. I think I might know him but I'm not sure. I don't trust him somehow. If he wants to buy, he should have made up his mind by now.'

Bella entered quietly, her heart hammering. If this was an intruder, with no intention of buying, aiming instead to cause trouble, she had no idea how she would deal with him. If her father had been there...

'If you need any help,' she said, her voice far more confident than she felt, 'please tell me, won't you?'

The man, who had been staring into the deep-freeze cabinets, turned round and with a jolt Bella recognised him. Oh, no, she thought, anyone but him.

'Mr Haddern,' she said, in her helpful shop assistant's tone, 'over there you'll find a basket for any items you collect as you go round.'

It seemed he hadn't come to shop. 'So, Bella,' his small eyes looked out of a full-cheeked face, 'we meet again.' Never before, she thought, had anyone turned her first name into an insult. 'My mother buys all the food I need, thanks, but I'll take a packet of those.' He pointed to the shop's stock of cigarettes out of his reach behind the small check-out and named a brand. As he paid, he looked her over insolently, unfastening the pack and extracting one, proceeding to light it.

'Sorry, Mr Haddern——' Bella indicated the 'No smoking' notices posted around the walls. He followed her eyes but it was as if she hadn't spoken. He continued, aiming the smoke, Bella was certain, straight at her face.

'Tell me, Bella,' he said, his smile none too pleasant, 'First Vernon Canford, then Jimmy—how do you do it?'

Bella wished another customer would come in, or even that Polly would interrupt with a question.

'Do what, Mr Haddern?' she asked as politely as she could.

He didn't answer, but his knowing eyes conveyed his meaning.

'If there's anything else you want, Mr Haddern,' Bella tried to keep her temper, 'just tell me, and I'll——'

'Got an evening free? Book me in your diary, Bella, between the Canford brothers. Not forgetting Reece, of course. That is, if you've got any energy to spare after they've——'

'I wouldn't make a date with you, Mr Haddern,' Bella retorted, 'if I had every day free from one New Year's Day to the next.'

Malcolm's face darkened. He stubbed out his cigarette, drew in his lips and slammed the shop door behind him.

'I thought I knew him!' Polly exclaimed. 'Wasn't it that awful Malcolm Haddern? Friend of the Strangor-Denmans? Lives on the other side of the town?'

Bella nodded and Polly made a face.

'Wouldn't trust him an inch, Bella. Hope he doesn't pay you back somehow for what you said to him.'

'What can he do?' Bella commented, dusting the rickety till and attempting to bring a shine to the worn wooden counter. 'It's Reece Denman who's done his worst to this business, taken my father away...' Turning, she rearranged some packets behind her, unwilling to let Polly see the despair that had been gripping her since seeing the eager faces of Columbine's customers that morning, and the attractive and compelling displays in the reopened store.

Custom at Food Fare picked up slowly as the week went by, the familiar faces drifting back, but Bella guessed by the snippets of conversation she heard in the shop that her customers were supplementing their purchases by patronising Columbine's.

One morning when the shop was empty a man entered, appearing to consider each footstep as if he might be walking across a minefield. Wary and retiring though he seemed, the look in his eyes was authoritative and determined.

'Is Mr Harrison available, please, Mr Edgar Harrison? My name is Fisher,' he held out an identification card, 'Harold Fisher, environmental health officer.'

Heart sinking, Bella explained her father's absence. 'I'm in charge, now, Mr Fisher, but——' Hand shaking a little, she indicated that the shop was his to inspect. She knew it was not within her power to refuse permission.

He nodded a little absent-mindedly, wandering round, carrying on even as customers came and went. All the while, Bella was conscious of his every pause, her anxiety mounting at each note he made.

Polly openly watched him, making faces behind his back and doing her best to pass the inspection off as a nuisance and a joke. It was no joke when the inspector, choosing a few quiet moments, approached the checkout with an expressionless face and asked quietly, 'Is there somewhere that we can talk?'

Half an hour later, Bella escorted him from the rear office to the shop door, closing it and turning the 'Open' sign around.

'Hey, Bella,' Polly exclaimed, 'there's twenty minutes to go before we shut!'

Bella shook her head, then put her hand to it. 'We're in trouble, Polly, big trouble. Someone's reported us for being below standard.'

'But who could have done such a rotten thing without telling us first, giving us a chance to put things right?'

Bella shook her head. She had her suspicions, but if she as much as mentioned his name she was sure she would explode. The evening she had fallen from the ladder and Reece had looked around the shop as they had waited for the doctor—that was when he must have seen all the shop's shortcomings. Hadn't she seen them for herself as she had lain there, secretly horrified at everything she saw from floor-level?

Bella sighed. 'There's such a long list of things to put right in such a short time, I just don't know how—or even if—I'm going to be able to do it. New shelving, new flooring, new frozen food cabinets, new almost everything. It's money I need, Polly, money I haven't got.'

'The bank?' Polly suggested tentatively.

Bella shrugged. 'What can we offer as security?'

Polly looked around hopelessly. 'If the money can't be found,' she whispered, 'what then?'

'It'll be the end of Harrison's Food Fare. If we don't carry out their recommendations, the inspector said, within the time limits they've set us, they'll close the shop.'

CHAPTER SIX

EDGAR eased off his shoes and leaned back in his favourite chair.

'Whew,' he pretended to mop his brow, 'I've never worked so hard in my life.' Bella's hopes rose sky-high. Was her father regretting his decision to work at Columbine's, and would he now announce that he was coming back to Food Fare? Her hopes came crashing as her father added, 'But I love it. The work, I mean.'

He turned to her. 'The opening was grand, lass. Pity you couldn't come.' So if even her father hadn't recognised her, then she could rest assured that Reece would not have done. 'The place was crowded, Bella.'

I know, she almost said. 'It seemed to have an effect on sales in our shop, Dad,' she remarked with assumed casualness. 'I think everyone must have gone to Columbine's opening ceremony.' Her smile was forced.

'I think they must,' Edgar answered, his smile genuine.

I've lost him well and truly, Bella thought, sadness sweeping over her. He identifies so much with his new job and his new employer that the fortunes of the shop he ran for all those years doesn't concern him any more.

'The environmental health officer visited the shop today, Dad,' she told him bluntly, but to her disappointment the impact of her words was not as great as she had secretly hoped.

'Did he, lass?' he commented with a detached interest. 'We haven't had an inspection for years. Did he approve of what he saw?'

'No, Dad, he didn't.' Bella told him then all that the inspector had said, producing the list he had left with her. She was relieved that she had her father's full attention at last.

'What am I going to do, Dad? Where am I going to get the money from to deal with all those things on that list?' Her voice was thick with emotion, the tears barely held at bay.

'Oh, dear me.' Edgar shook his head slowly and stared unseeingly at the potted plant that filled the old-fashioned grate.

'There's Reece,' he said at last. 'You could go and ask him if his take-over offer still stands.'

'Reece Denman the wonder man,' she said acidly, 'who can wave a wand and all your dreams will come true. Who can pour gold—or, in this case, cash—into your pockets until they're spilling over, then you can buy your way out of all your difficulties?'

'Don't be bitter, lass,' her father urged. 'He's not so bad for one who's come from the other end of the town.'

But Bella hadn't finished. 'Ask Reece, when I'm certain he was the one who informed on us to the inspectorate?' At her father's look of astonished disbelief, she insisted, 'It must have been him.' She told her father how Reece had wandered round the shop the evening she had injured herself. 'He did it to spite me because I opposed Strong Nation taking over Food Fare. Dad,' she added after a short silence, 'I'm terribly worried. I just don't know what to do.'

'Don't upset yourself,' Edgar said, leaning forward and patting his daughter's hand, 'I'll think of something. Just give me time.'

Had she really thought that her father might say, I'll leave Columbine's and come back into the business?

'That's something we haven't got,' Bella pointed out unhappily. She told her father just how short a time the inspector had given her.

'Oh, my,' he commented, leaning back, eyes anxious now. For a while they sat in silence, then Edgar declared, 'There's some savings I put aside for a rainy day, dear. You could have the money now.'

Bella was almost moved to tears by her father's offer. She shook her head. 'Thanks, Dad, but it wouldn't even scratch the surface.'

'Leave it to me,' he said confidently. 'I'll find a way.'

After a pause, Bella heard herself say, quite against her conscious will, 'I'd . . . I think I'd even go to Reece for help, if it came to a choice between closing down and staying open. It'd be an awful pill to swallow, Dad, asking him for help, but——' Her shoulders lifted and fell.

'I don't know what you've got against him, Bella. As far as my opinion of him's concerned, he's the salt of the earth.'

Bella sighed, unconvinced. 'Oh, he can put on the charm when he likes, but I can see through it. It's false and shallow, Dad. Underneath, he's as hard as granite.' Her father was shaking his head as Bella insisted, 'He *has* to be to have got where he is.'

Three precious days went by, days of inaction during which Bella had been at war with herself.

That morning, Polly asked dejectedly, 'What's going to happen, Bella? Is the shop closing after all? I must know soon, you see, because I'll have to find another job.'

The question brought Bella face to face at last with the inevitable. Her own prejudice against the only person who could help her was affecting, not only her own future, but that of her assistant.

She had to make up her mind. No matter how she might have to eat her words, nor how it might grind her pride into the dust, somehow she would have to find a way of seeing Reece and pleading her case.

It was when their evening meal was behind them, as Bella and her father relaxed in the living-room, that he dropped two bombshells. The impacts were explosive and Bella reeled under the shock-waves.

'Do you recall my telling you,' Edgar remarked with a casualness which, knowing her father as she did, Bella was certain was assumed, 'that Reece had purchased a number of flats in the town to house some of his more senior employees?'

'He'd offered you one, and you turned it down. I remember.' She too had put on a casual act, because she guessed what was coming. 'You've—you're going to tell me you've changed your mind and accepted?'

'I wondered if——' he leaned back, but his movements were unrelaxed and worried '—if you'd have any objections to my saying yes, dear?'

Although she had half expected it, when it actually came it shook her world to its foundations. It was a blow from which she needed a few moments to recover.

'Of—of course not, Dad,' she answered at last, eliminating by sheer will-power the tremor from her voice. 'But——' she cleared her throat '—but who'll look after you, cook your meals...?'

'Well,' Edgar shifted as though he couldn't find a comfortable position, 'Reece has been good enough to ask Maddy Langridge if she'd oblige in that respect and she accepted gladly, he said.'

'That's—that's just great!' Bella exclaimed, congratulating herself on her acting ability.

'All the same, it worries me a bit, leaving you alone here. You'll be all right at night? You're sure?'

Bella laughed. 'I'm a big girl now, Dad. I'll be fine. And I can understand your wanting to live in a—a nicer place than this, now you've got such a good job.'

'It's not that, lass. It's just that it'll be so much more convenient living nearer the store when I work evenings. Columbine's stays open late on certain days, and you might not believe it but even the short drive here I find tiring. There's another thing, Bella. I spoke to Reece about your problems.' He was silent for so long, Bella could hardly bear it.

'And...?'

Edgar shook his head. 'He can be very hard when he likes, can that lad.'

He's not a lad any more, she almost shouted. 'What did he say, Dad?'

Edgar frowned. 'He seemed angry about something. I got nowhere with him, nowhere at all.'

Well, she wouldn't have to find a way of seeing him now. She knew in advance the answer he would give to any appeal she might make to him for help. She knew the reason for his anger, too. Her head rang with her own defiant and, as she now had to acknowledge, foolish declaration to Reece on the subject.

'You'd be the last person I'd turn to,' she had defiantly declared the evening he had insisted on escorting her home after Jimmy's dog had run away. 'The sort of help I might need, and I hope I never do, wouldn't be the kind you would offer.'

Could she blame him now if he'd said an unequivocal 'no' to her father's appeal on her behalf?

'Am I imagining it, Polly, or is a miracle happening?' Bella queried next day as a customer left with a wave. 'Are the old faces coming back to the fold?'

A lady customer had just pleaded, 'Don't close, Miss Harrison, lots of us like Food Fare best.'

'Maybe you're right, Bella, maybe you're not,' Polly answered doubtfully. 'But it's not much use now, is it, since we've got to close?'

Bella held up crossed fingers. 'I still keep hoping.' She didn't tell Polly that it was a vain hope. Her father had promised to try the bank once more, but he'd sighed as he had said it.

'Bella, old pal!' Jacqueline erupted into view, setting the shop bell joyfully ringing. 'Just had to tell you. Dick and I have bought a house.'

'That's great,' Bella said, delighted to see her friend again.

'Next week I move in. There's decorating to do, measuring up... you know? You must come and see it soon. Now,' she looked at the piece of paper in her hand, 'I've got a list of wants as long as your arm.' She put it on the counter. 'Can do?'

'Most of them, luckily.'

'Good old Harrison's stores,' remarked Jacqueline. 'Always did turn up trumps. It's the "cupboard is bare" syndrome at home, and I refuse to go ears down to my brother's palatial superstore. Without realising, I let the basic necessities run down a bit while Dick was around, and my dear brother's begun to grumble at the meals his little sister's been serving up. Not that he pays me to be his housekeeper. When Dick and I marry he'll have to get someone to do his cooking, not to mention ironing and washing and... But I'm boring you.'

For a few moments she watched Bella seeking and finding and piling the goods on the counter. 'I'm feeling lonely, Bella.' She turned her mouth down. 'Dick's gone off to Paris on business. Come over this afternoon?'

Bella's face lit up. It was Saturday and Polly could take over. Custom on summer Saturdays often slackened off. Anyway, since her father had left to live in his new home she too had been feeling lonely. Then she remembered where her friend lived and shook her head.

Jacqueline frowned and asked in a hurt tone, 'What's wrong? Have you put me outside your circle of acquaintances or something, just because I'm engaged?'

'No, no, of course not. It's——' It's because I don't want to meet your brother. How could she tell Jacqueline that?

If Jacqueline had not managed to read her friend's mind, she had certainly read her expression. 'If it's Reece you're worried about, even if he's there, which he might not be, he won't invade my part of the house. It's mine, he said, until I marry. So?'

Still Bella hesitated.

Deflated, Jacqueline asked, 'Could you get Robbie Hardcastle to deliver this lot, Bella? I'm going home to mope for Dick and watch boring films and——'

'I'll deliver these, Jacqueline,' Bella broke in. 'I don't...I can't afford to employ Robbie any more.'

'You can't?' A frown of sympathy, then a smile. 'OK, pal, you deliver and I'll grab your ignition keys so you can't come back here until I let you. How's that for friendship?'

Bella laughed, packing her friend's groceries neatly.

Bella balanced the box of groceries on one upraised knee, rang the bell and heard footsteps approach.

'Come round into the garden,' Jacqueline yelled from a distance. 'I'm sunning myself by the pool. Just leave the box on the steps. I'll bring it in later.'

The front door swung wide. Reece's eyes flickered with something like surprise mixed with—was it irritation? It had to be, hadn't it, Bella reasoned, because, he was probably thinking, of all people, he had found *her* on the doorstep?

Her arms hugged the box which was growing heavier by the second.

'Sorry,' her head went up, 'I've come to the wrong door. You're going to tell me that deliveries and tradespeople should go round the back. So I won't wait to be told.'

She started to turn when arms shot out and, none too gently, wrested the box from her.

'There was no need,' she protested, 'I've grown quite used to lifting heavy loads. The muscles in my arms,' she held her biceps out for his inspection, 'have grown really strong since I took over the running of my shop. My shop,' she repeated with a defiant stare.

His answering gaze told her nothing. It moved slowly from her arms to contemplate the area of fair skin which her low-cut sun-dress revealed, descending over the gentle swell which pushed impudently at the floral fabric, then down, down over her hips to her bare legs and skimpily sandalled feet.

'That your working gear?' The down-putting question grazed her sensibilities and a slow blush turned her skin's pallor as red as if his words had really scraped it.

She went to snatch the box back, but a half-turn put it out of her reach.

'Bella!' Jacqueline shouted impatiently. She shot round the side of the building, came to a surprised halt, summed up the situation and groaned. 'I might have known. Reece,' she commanded, 'leave my old friend alone. You keep to your part of the house and I'll entertain who I like in mine. That was the arrangement we agreed to.'

Imperious eyebrows lifted, possessing the ability, it seemed, to crush even a sister. 'Since when has access to the front entrance door been the prerogative of only one of us?'

'OK, I apologise. But I wish you'd stop *bullying* Bella whenever you come into contact with her.'

'Contact?' Those eyebrows shot up this time, topping two mocking, evaluating eyes and a sardonically curved mouth. 'That'll be the day.' It was obvious to Bella, if not to her friend, what kind of 'contact' Reece had in mind. It wasn't, she was only too well aware, of a social, nor of a business nature.

Jacqueline eyed the box in his arms. 'I'll unpack those groceries later. You see,' with a cheeky grin at her brother, 'I still shop at the little shop on the corner. You can *keep* your exotic palaces erected to the great god "Food". Not to mention, Mammon.'

'Yeah?' her brother responded, going back through the years to their companionable if skirmishing younger days. 'So was it your double I saw the other day wandering dreamily round Columbine's, filling her basket as fast as she could with caviare and fresh salmon?'

'OK, I surrender.' Jacqueline took Bella's arm. 'Columbine's might be great in a lot of ways, but there's one thing it hasn't got.' She swung her friend's arm high like a referee presenting a victorious boxer. 'Bella Harrison. She's the best sales lady I've ever come across. In that box are half a dozen things I bought on her recommendation, although I didn't really need them. OK, brother dear?'

She tugged Bella round the corner and out of sight.

'Now,' she ordered, 'put yourself right there,' she patted an air-bed, 'and for heaven's sake, relax. You look all on edge. Tell Auntie Jacqueline. Pretend it's a psychiatrist's couch.' She lay back, like Bella, on her own air-bed. 'Now, I'm all ears.'

Fifteen minutes later, she turned on her side, staring at her friend. 'It's as bad as that? And it's money you need?'

'Fast.'

For some time, Jacqueline was silent. 'There's got to be some way,' she said at length, 'of changing my dear brother's mind.'

'Don't *you* ask him on my behalf,' Bella pleaded anxiously. 'First my father, then you.'

'*Me* ask him? Are you crazy? No. This time, it's got to be you.'

Bella stared up into the blue sky. She had slipped off the straps of her sun-dress so as to brown her shoulders after coating them with sun-screen.

'I couldn't,' she said at last. 'I've thought about it, but after the awful things I've said to him——'

'Think about it again, Bella. Your father's tried the bank once more, but—brick-wall stuff, yes? So, one more try with R Strangor-Denman junior—isn't it worth eating your pride for?'

Bella sighed. 'I just don't know. Vernon and Jimmy, they've been so sweet. They offered me their savings on a long-term interest-free basis but I just couldn't accept. Anyway,' sadly, 'the amount wouldn't have been enough.'

It was Jacqueline's turn to sigh. She rolled on to her back again and shielded her eyes from the sun. There was a thoughtful silence. 'There's just got to be a way,' she said at last, 'of getting through to my brother just how serious your situation is.'

Bella gave a slow, emphatic dismissal of her friend's suggestion, but Jacqueline would not be deflected. There was no doubting, Bella decided wryly, that she had in her a large helping of her brother's stubbornness.

Jacqueline sat up, twisting to look her friend over.

'Bella, dear, you've got what it takes, you've got everything Marguerite Hunter-Parkes has got, plus, unlike her, you've got it here, too.' She tapped her head. 'If you really wanted, you could get my brother in the palm of your hand.'

Bella laughed. 'Twist him round my little finger, you mean?'

Jacqueline grinned. 'One good cliché deserves another.'

'But what,' Bella queried, 'would I do with him after that? No, don't answer. So I know what some girls would do, but I'm not made like that. Despite what some people might think, what's between Vernon and Jimmy and me is *friendship*, pure and simple. I swear, Jacqueline——'

Jacqueline held up her hand. 'D'you think I believed all those rumours? I know you better than that. Anyway, I've seen Vernon out with Mary Walker who works at Smith's, the newsagents. Did you know?'

'It's OK, Vernon told me he likes her.'

'That's all right, then.' Another sigh and she sank back. 'Reece has pots of money. I know he's worked hard for it and deserves it, but somehow you've got to find a way of persuading some of it out of him, use of feminine wiles or not.' She sat up, patting her mouth. 'I'm dying for a drink. Non-alcoholic, yes? Come on, let's raid the fridge and I'll see what I can find.'

Bella trotted after her friend, running fingers through her tousled hair and inspecting her arms for any colour change and hoping that Jacqueline's brother was on the other side of that very large house and couldn't see them.

'Here we are, home-made lemonade. I made it this morning.' Jacqueline produced a jug, which she peered into. 'Reece's favourite. Hey, he hasn't left us much. Reece, you moron. You've almost drunk the well dry.'

Bella, heart racing from walking-pace to Olympic speeds, swung round. He was there filling the doorway, arm upraised, other hand arrogantly on hip, a sardonic smile playing over his lips. His navy knitted shirt hugged his torso, while his jeans sat low on the ridge of his hips.

Jacqueline handed Bella a filled glass and lifted hers to Bella in a kind of toast. She took a drink and, holding Bella's gaze, moved the glass infinitesimally in Reece's direction. Go on, Jacqueline was urging, his mood's OK. Tell him now.

Sending a look of appeal to her friend, Bella moistened her lips, then swung her eyes to Reece. 'I——' Why was her voice so hoarse? She cleared her throat. 'I wonder if——'

Reece, his mind seemingly occupied with Bella's throat and bared shoulders, continued to lean against the door-frame, giving her no help at all.

Jacqueline, plainly impatient with her friend's hesitant manner, said bluntly, 'Reece, Bella wants your help.'

'She does? That's news.' His tone implied that it wasn't news at all. 'So?'

The question this time was directed at Bella.

'It's—oh, for heaven's sake, Reece,' Jacqueline answered for her, 'come off your high horse. Bella's got a problem——' Reece's eyebrows shot up and his eyes beneath them did a survey of Bella's curves. 'No, not that, you idiot. She can manage her private life without your help. It's *financial*. She's in dire trouble.'

'I heard. She wouldn't accept her boyfriends'—in the plural—offer to hand over their savings to her.'

'You horrible spy! You must have crept up behind us while we were talking. Why didn't you let us know you were there?'

'I didn't want to interrupt the flow of girlish chatter.'

'How condescending can a brother get?' Jacqueline asked exasperatedly.

'I came out to ask if you'd like me to bring you out a drink. The words that really riveted me were something about your friend "eating her pride".'

'Whoops,' said Jacqueline, hand over mouth, 'oh, dear. Over to you, pal. See you back at the pool.' She made her escape.

'Please don't go, Jacqueline,' Bella called desperately, but her friend had vanished.

'So why,' Reece asked, hands in trouser pockets, 'were you going to have to "eat your pride"?'

'That's my business,' she answered stiffly. 'I don't have to answer.'

He looked at her steadily and Bella filled the prickling silence by drinking her lemonade and going to the sink to rinse the empty glass. There was a movement behind her, then Reece's breath fanned over her skin. She shivered involuntarily and tried to move away but his solid presence proved too large an obstacle.

'You're very much at home in my house,' he drawled, so near to her ear that she jumped, 'despite the fact that you despise it as being symbolic of my belonging to the moneyed class. In accepting my sister's invitation to come here, weren't you going against your principles?'

With jerky movements, she upended the glass to drain and swung out of his tormenting orbit by lifting the towel from the rail and drying her hands.

He had hit a sensitive spot and it hurt. It was true that something inside her still strongly resented the relative ease in which he lived as compared with her and her father's way of life, except that her father was living a life of greater comfort now than ever before. Thanks, reminded a small voice, to this man's benevolence.

'Jacqueline's my friend,' she declared, facing him, head back because he was so tall. 'She has been for years. Friendship, in my opinion, breaks down class barriers.'

'So friendship, you're saying, is your means of access to the world of the better off on which you've always poured scorn and to a house you've always condemned for being on the "other"—that is, richer—side of the town?' Bella turned away, replacing the towel. His hands caught at her bare upper arms and swung her back. 'Now that is really what I call hypocritical.'

'All right, so you don't like me,' she said with a false belligerence. 'But I'm not asking you to. All I'm asking is——' *No!* screeched that voice inside her head. But nothing could recall the words and he was on to them like a baited trap snapping a mouse.

His fingers dug into her arms but she would not plead for mercy. 'Yes?' he asked over-smoothly. 'All you're asking is——?'

'Nothing,' she retorted. 'I wouldn't ask anything of you, you who informed on me to the authorities and got me into the mess I'm in.'

His arms dropped to his sides. 'That *I* got you in? You think that I would sink so low as to expose you to the inspectorate without first telling you I was doing so, and why?'

Rubbing her arms where he had held her, Bella caught her breath. 'You mean it—it wasn't you? But that evening I fell off the step-ladder, you wandered round the shop. You must have seen all its shortcomings.'

'I saw. The old fitments, the dirt traps, the bad state of the place. I tried to figure out how much cash would be required to bring the place up to standard.'

Bella frowned. 'But you didn't——?'

'No, I did not. Instead, I made an offer which would have involved buying out the business, an idea which delighted your father, but which he eventually—and reluctantly—refused because his daughter, whom he loves dearly, gave it the thumbs down.'

'If you didn't tell the authorities,' Bella persisted, 'then who did?'

'Still not convinced? All right, I'll tell you. Malcolm Haddern.' Yes! she thought. Polly told me how he'd wandered round the shop for ages, inspecting every nook and cranny.

'Malcolm told me,' Reece went on, '*after* he'd contacted them.'

'But why? Of course! To pay me back because I refused him a date. And now,' her voice thickened with tears, 'because of him, because of your *friend*, my shop's been condemned as a health hazard, and there's nothing I can do about it because I simply don't have the money to put it right. That's your close acquaintances for you, Mr Strangor-Denman, your wonderful *friends*. Informers, squealers, spies——'

'That's enough.' He caught her to him. 'By God, I'll shut that beautiful, *abusive* mouth of yours.' His hand gathered her hair, tugging her head back and placing his mouth on hers in a cruel and unrelenting kiss.

Slowly, as her body unwillingly succumbed to his dominance, and despite the pain he was inflicting on her head, she felt all resistance ebbing from her. Of their own accord her arms lifted to link around his neck. When her breasts began to tingle and throb she realised with a shock that his hands must have pushed down the top of her sun-dress where the lowered shoulder straps had left her vulnerable to his audacious invasion.

Under his persuasive caresses, every nerve in her body began to ache, her lips willingly parting to accept his intrusion, her breaths coming and going in strangled grasps.

Without warning, he jerked her clinging mouth free of his, his eyes grazing her inflamed flesh, lingering on her pouting nipples and burgeoning shape, then back to her eyes where he read the message she could not hide: I want you to make love to me, take me any time you like.

His lips curved in a cynical, mirthless smile, then with a movement that was almost an insult he thrust her from him.

Bella, drained and as humiliated as he had intended her to be, with trembling fingers put her dress to rights. His fast-fading footsteps took him out of the house and into his car which fired to life and roared away down the drive.

CHAPTER SEVEN

IT WAS Sunday afternoon and Bella stared down into the half-empty street and forced herself to face reality.

The time the authorities had allowed her for replacing all her old, substandard fittings with modern equipment had almost passed. Yet she was no nearer to fulfilling their instructions than when they had first issued them.

Yesterday, she reproached herself, she had had the chance of personally seeking Reece's help, yet by her outburst had ruined everything. He had been her last hope. Now, despite her efforts to keep the business going, she was finally facing defeat.

She read again the note that Polly had left and which she had found in the office on her return from her evening with Jacqueline.

'Stay to a meal,' her friend had begged. 'I know you had a row with my dear brother. I could hear your voices—not what you said, I hasten to add. But it isn't the end of the world. Anyway, I heard him go out, which means he's gone to join his lady-friend Marguerite.'

Where else? Bella thought unhappily. I should have guessed that that was where he'd gone. The kisses he gave me meant no more to him than as a very male and macho way of inflicting punishment on a female who'd aroused his anger as much as I had.

'He won't be back for hours,' Jacqueline had assured her, 'maybe not this side of tomorrow, so you needn't worry about him bullying you again today. Ring Polly, there's a pal, and tell her to lock up or whatever. You can trust her to do that, can't you?'

This Bella had done, after initial hesitation. Polly, she'd thought, had sounded a little strained, but she'd dismissed the idea, reasoning that, at the end of the day, her assistant was probably tired.

'Dear Bella,' the note said, 'when you phoned, I couldn't tell you that Mr Denman was here, because he told me not to.'

So, Bella thought, he hadn't gone to see his lady-friend as Jacqueline had guessed.

'He went into the office,' Polly's note went on, 'and asked me where the key to the filing cabinet was. I said I didn't know if I should, and he said it was OK, because he was here to help you. So I gave it to him. He read through all those cash books, Bella, and made lots of notes. Then he looked over the shop, which was when you phoned. Then he thanked me and went off. Hope it was OK doing what I did, but I trusted him because, well, somehow you do, don't you? Trust Mr Denman, I mean. See you Monday. Love, Polly.'

Tossing the note on to a table, Bella sighed, her eyes bleak, her heart heavy. So Reece would have seen everything, the falling sales, the calculations she had done to try to balance the books, the correspondence her father had had with the bank. All in vain.

When the telephone rang, she jumped. For a few moments, she just stared at it, then, since it hadn't stopped, she trod towards it warily, and lifted the receiver without speaking.

'Bella.' She'd known all along, she admitted to herself, who it was. She did not respond. 'Bella? I know you're there. I can hear you breathing.' She held her breath. 'Bella!' It was a command and with a frightening growl mixed in. Still receiving no reply, the caller rammed the receiver into place, making Bella's eardrum reverberate and her heart dive in at the deep end, never, she was certain, to surface again.

There goes my very last hope of all, she thought, her hand shaking as it replaced her own receiver, a mind change on Reece's part.

She pulled on a sweatshirt and fresh cotton trousers, slipping on her walking shoes. Then she dipped her head against the strong breeze and set out for the fields.

A car screeched to a stop at the kerbside and a hand reached out to grab her arm. 'I've come to talk to you.'

'I don't want to talk to *you*,' was her defiant, and, to her annoyance, tremulous answer. She knew it was because her nerves were as taut as stretched elastic and her sleep had lately been troubled and restless.

He released her and she walked on, arms stiffly to her sides so that he could not grab them again. She had reckoned without his dogged persistence. He kept pace, driving slowly. 'OK,' he clipped, 'if that's the way you want it, you walk, I drive, we'll talk. Let's see who gets arrested first: me for kerb crawling or you for soliciting.'

'*Me?*' Her face flooded with indignant colour. 'You mean——?'

'Importuning. Yes.' He leaned even further across, his gaze doing an instant survey of her shape. Hooded eyes lifted to hers, a tautly male mouth commented, 'You've got what it takes. A man couldn't be blamed for——'

'Will you be quiet?'

A passer-by raised her eyebrows at the scene, tutting to herself. Bella, more embarrassed than ever, stopped in her tracks. '*Please*, Reece, will you leave me alone?'

He braked. 'That's better,' he said, hearing the unintentional note of capitulation. 'Get in. Come what may, we're *talking*, understand?

'I don't want to talk,' her lips said stiffly, but her brain reprimanded their continuing recalcitrance. You want—you *need*—to talk to this man more than anything, or anyone, in the world, it said. Her hand opened the door, and the rest of her followed its co-operative example, sliding into the passenger seat.

Reece shot her a look of grim satisfaction and, turning the wheel, joined the traffic flow. 'We're heading for the Duke's Park,' he informed her, and lapsed into a silence that persisted for the rest of the journey.

At the impressive stone-arched gate, Reece paid the entry fee and drove to the parking area, bumping over grassland to line up neatly beside other cars.

All around, the privately owned park, which was open to the public, stretched into the far distance. Bella, like many others from the surrounding districts, knew it well, having walked and played in it from childhood on.

The great palace, with its ornate style and enclosed landscaped gardens which the park lovingly cosseted, had been built in the early eighteenth century.

For some time they walked in silence, descending a little and halting to stare across the lake magically conceived and designed by Lancelot 'Capability' Brown, and admiring Vanbrugh's Grand Bridge with a story all its own.

'I've got a proposition to make,' Reece said at last, his eyes on the sun's rippling reflection and the graceful trees that adorned the wide stretch of water.

What was coming now? Bella wondered, her hopes of receiving any true help from him dwindling to nil.

'Contrary to what you may be thinking,' he added on a mocking note, 'it's business I have in mind. No dishonourable overtones. Do I,' his hand lifted, touching her cheek, 'have your ear, as they say?' In a familiar gesture, his long fingers pushed her hair aside and traced a caressing line around that part of her, flicking the swinging gilt earring that shone in the sunlight.

'I can hear you,' she remarked, deliberately deadpan to conceal the shivering excitement his touch never failed to arouse. Raising her head, she smiled. 'I've retuned

my internal listening device to receive your pearls of
wisdom.'

He reached round and sharply tapped her rear.
'Impudent minx.'

'That,' she retorted, rubbing where his hand had inflicted its punishment, 'couldn't be interpreted as
"business" in any language.'

'OK, so don't provoke.'

They continued walking, making for the ancient
arched stone bridge and hearing tourists expressing in
their own many and varied tongues their enjoyment of
the scene. Occasionally Reece took Bella's hand to pull
her out of other people's photographs.

They found a raised step and leaned on the parapet
of the bridge, their hips touching in the minuscule space
provided by the bay. Coots swam and dived, disap-
pearing in their search for food, great crested grebes
moved graciously through reflected clouds and blue sky,
while Canada geese glided smoothly through the water,
honking incongruously to their mates.

'I'm willing,' Reece said over the mingling voices of
visitors and children's squeals and laughter, 'to help you
solve your problems regarding Food Fare.'

'Are you saying,' her voice rose eagerly, 'that you'll
lend me the money I need to put right all the things that
the inspector says are wrong with it?'

'Not so fast,' he cautioned sharply. A pause in which,
for Bella, time seemed to stand still. 'No,' he finished
decisively.

The seconds raced on again, carrying away with them
all Bella's hopes.

'It would go against the grain,' Reece enlarged, coldly
detached, 'to prop up a business by throwing money, as
it were, into a bottomless pit. Which is what it would
amount to if Food Fare were to be refitted to the standard
required by the authorities.'

NO RISK, NO OBLIGATION TO BUY ... NOW OR EVER!

CASINO JUBILEE
"Scratch'n Match" Game

Here's how to play:

1. Peel off label from front cover. Place it in space provided at right. With a coin, carefully scratch off the silver box. This makes you eligible to receive two or more free books, and possibly other gifts, depending upon what is revealed beneath the scratch-off area.

2. You'll receive brand-new Harlequin Presents® novels. When you return this card, we'll rush you the books and gifts you qualify for, ABSOLUTELY FREE!

3. If we don't hear from you, every month we'll send you 6 additional novels to read and enjoy months before they are available in bookstores. You can return them and owe nothing, but if you decide to keep them, you'll pay only $2.49* per book, a saving of 40¢ each off the cover price. There is **no** extra charge for postage and handling. There are **no** hidden extras.

4. When you join the Harlequin Reader Service®, you'll get our subscribers-only newsletter, as well as additional free gifts from time to time, just for being a subscriber!

5. You must be completely satisfied. You may cancel at any time simply by sending us a note or a shipping statement marked "cancel" or by returning any shipment to us at our cost.

YOURS FREE!

This lovely heart-shaped box is richly detailed with cut-glass decorations, perfect for holding a precious memento or keepsake—and it's yours absolutely free when you accept our no-risk offer.

CASINO JUBILEE
"Scratch'n Match" Game

SCRATCH HERE

PLACE LABEL HERE

?

CHECK CLAIM CHART BELOW
FOR YOUR FREE GIFTS!

YES! I have placed my label from the front cover in the space provided above and scratched off the silver box. Please send me all the gifts for which I qualify. I understand I am under no obligation to purchase any books, as explained on the opposite page.

(U-H-P-08/92) 106 CIH AFN9

Name _____

Address _____ Apt. _____

City _____ State _____ Zip _____

CASINO JUBILEE CLAIM CHART

🍒🍒🍒	WORTH 4 FREE BOOKS, FREE HEART-SHAPED CURIO BOX PLUS MYSTERY BONUS GIFT
🍒🔔🍒	WORTH 3 FREE BOOKS PLUS MYSTERY GIFT
🔔🔔🍒	WORTH 2 FREE BOOKS CLAIM N° 1528

◄ DETACH AND MAIL CARD TODAY! ◄

HARLEQUIN ''NO RISK'' GUARANTEE

- You're not required to buy a single book—ever!
- You must be completely satisfied or you may cancel at any time simply by sending us a note or a shipping statement marked ''cancel'' or by returning any shipment to us at our cost. Either way, you will receive no more books; you'll have no obligation to buy.
- The free books and gift(s) you claimed on the ''Casino Jubilee'' offer remain yours to keep no matter what you decide.

If offer card is missing, please write to: Harlequin Reader Service® P.O. Box 1867, Buffalo, N.Y. 14269-1867

◆ DETACH AND MAIL CARD TODAY! ◆

BUSINESS REPLY MAIL
FIRST CLASS MAIL   PERMIT NO. 717   BUFFALO, NY

POSTAGE WILL BE PAID BY ADDRESSEE

HARLEQUIN READER SERVICE
3010 WALDEN AVE
PO BOX 1867
BUFFALO NY 14240-9952

NO POSTAGE
NECESSARY
IF MAILED
IN THE
UNITED STATES

'You mean,' Bella said bitterly, 'you're too slick and clever a businessman to throw good money after bad.'

'I could,' he commented grimly, 'take exception to your description, but I won't. And the answer's yes.'

'So we're back to a buy-out, a *take-over*, in fact.'

'We are.'

'And,' tentatively because it would be too wonderful to be true, 'you'd subsidise the business, let it carry on?'

'Sorry to tread on your dreams, but no.'

'You mean—a close down?'

'A close-down.'

Temper flared like a flame to paper. 'Then you can *keep* your offer, your useless *proposition!*' She made to step down and move away but checked herself, returning to lean on the parapet.

After a long and painful silence, she whispered, 'I'm sorry. I didn't mean to throw your offer of help back in your face again, but——' She fought with herself, reluctant to be forced on to the defensive, but her deepest feelings had begun to struggle to the surface. How could she convey to this hard-headed businessman that ordinary human emotions also played a part in the world—her world—of commerce?

'All right,' she admitted at last, 'so I operate on a very narrow profit margin. Also, I'm only able to employ help in the shop because Polly's willing to take less than she'd get elsewhere.' Another long pause.

Reece, apparently willing to give her all the time she needed to explain herself, yet unwilling to help her out, stared into the near distance, apparently absorbed by the graceful flight of swallows swooping through the warm air and skimming the water.

'People,' Bella went on, wondering if he was listening, 'come from all around just to shop at Food Fare. My father used to treat them as if they were his friends.'

'Now he's gone,' Reece intervened, showing that he had heard her after all, 'has it made a difference?'

'To the number of customers?' Bella was unwilling to admit that it had, but she had to be honest. 'Maybe. Or maybe——' She stopped, angry with herself for what she had so nearly conceded.

He turned inscrutable eyes to hers. 'Go on. Or maybe it's the effect of Columbine's revitalised appearance on the shopping scene?'

She was silent and his smile was touched with cynicism as he returned to his apparent preoccupation with the park's wildlife.

'People,' Bella declared, obliquely responding to his question, 'come to us from the surrounding villages rather than drive into town because that way they can avoid that awful traffic jam they have to contend with every time they go to Columbine's.'

'Nevertheless,' he responded drily, 'Columbine's pulling power has increased since its reopening.'

'Great for Columbine's,' she commented bitterly. 'But *I* do something your store doesn't. My customers don't have to line up at packed check-outs, trying to control their fretful kids, unpacking their stuff to be priced then having to pack it in shopping bags that spill over because they're too full. *I* deliver my customers' orders in my own car—after helping them pack the stuff. Sometimes they ask me in for a cup of tea. Sometimes, I drive a customer home along with her groceries, like my dad did.'

'OK, so you're telling me you've got the human touch.'

'There's no doubt about it. It's what's missing from life these days. I treat people as individuals, not just as a faceless line at a fantastically technological check-out.'

'Point taken.' His voice was brusque, but not, Bella was glad to note, dismissive. Was he giving her a chance, as well as a hearing?

Another tantalising silence, then, 'Reece?' She heard the waver, but it was there because she'd been so encouraged by his willingness to listen. 'Are you——?' She swallowed. 'Are you reconsidering——?'

'No.'

A long drawn-out sob escaped her throat and she backed down from the step, this time starting to make her way back over the bridge. A hand, whose grip she was beginning to know so well, grasped her shoulder, sliding down to hold her hand, entangling its fingers with hers so that she could not escape.

With his other hand he turned her face, looking into it, seeing the unhappiness there. His lips firmed and she thought he might abandon her on the spot, after which the whole subject would never be raised again. Then what would she do?

'Shall we walk?' She was propelled firmly towards the steep bank that overlooked and sloped down to the lake from another side.

Reece peeled off his sweater, spreading it on the grassy slope, seating himself and retrieving Bella's hand, tugging her down beside him. It reminded her of the evening they had met crossing the fields when he had removed his jacket to protect her shoulders from the rain. As she descended, with strong-muscled arms he halted her in mid-air. 'As long as you promise me,' he remarked with a lazy smile, 'not to fling *this* item of clothing back in my face.' Which meant that he had remembered, too.

After his jibe, having only checked her descent he allowed her downward plunge to continue and she toppled helplessly on to him. A shriek escaped her and she found herself sprawled face down over his hard thighs and sharp knees.

'For goodness' sake, help me up,' she cried.

His unrelenting hand held her down by her rear. 'Please,' she implored, her face scarlet at the indignity of her position.

'A forfeit for your freedom,' he tormented, rolling her over and across his knees. Before she could recover her poise, his hand spanned her throat and his mouth came down, imprisoning hers and making free with its moist sweetness until she gasped for mercy.

'Oh, boy,' a jarring voice broke into the breathless, unbelievably pleasurable moment, 'what have we here? The love-scene of the century. God, I wish I had my camera. Marguerite would have been livid if I'd been able to catch on film her man making love to a little shop girl.'

Bella, scarlet-faced, freed herself, sitting up and using trembling hands to tidy her hair.

'Malc, get,' Reece said languidly, remaining prone and cushioning his head with his upraised hands. Plainly his friend's mention of Marguerite's name hadn't disturbed him in the least.

Bella, recovering fast, glared up at the newcomer. His twisted expression made her shiver but she refused to allow him one single glimpse of her fear.

'Let me in on the act, Reece,' Malcolm pretended to plead. 'This lady must have something out of this world. She's got half the town going round in circles for her. The Canford brothers, lord of the manor Reece Denman himself, me if she'd so much as give me a flash of the old come-on...' He made to prod Reece with his foot. 'Move over, there's a pal, and let me sample——'

Reece's fist came down hard on his friend's toes. Malcolm let out a yelp and, with bad grace, went on his way.

'You might at least apologise,' Bella said, her cheeks still warm, her pride rallying to her aid.

Also, infuriating though Malcolm Haddern's innuendoes had been, his comments had served to remind her that Reece Denman was not emotionally free, that he had a lady-friend with oceans more to offer than Bella Harrison, financially struggling daughter of one of his employees. In addition to which, Marguerite's looks were fantastic, whereas hers...OK, she thought, I'm told I'm attractive, but what's that compared with stunning beauty?

'Apologise? Why?' Reece came upright beside her, his smile sardonic. 'We both enjoyed it. That you can't deny.'

To which remark she could find no answer. Had she really been stupid enough to attach any deeper meaning to a kiss which, on his part, had merely constituted a snatched moment of pleasure, of proving his physical dominance over her?

'You said you wanted to talk,' she reminded him, with a nonchalance she did not feel.

'Ah, yes.' His eyes were back contemplating the view, his manner having returned with alarming speed to detachment and neutrality. Which surely proved, Bella told herself, just how little that kiss *had* meant to him.

'If...' he was clearly choosing his words '...if nobody came to your aid, what would you do?'

She hugged her knees. 'You know that already. I honestly think you're gloating, that you don't really intend to try and help me.'

'Think what you like,' was his shrugging reply. 'So, the shutters would go up. End of Food Fare. End of the road for Harrison's.'

'Yes.'

'Bella.' A long pause, then, 'I'd be prepared to take a chance on you. I've given the matter a great deal of thought.'

Hardly daring to breathe, Bella waited, staring un-seeingly at the rippling waters below them.

'But it would be conditional,' he continued, 'on closing your shop.' He waited for her remonstrance, but her breathing difficulties continued to impede any kind of response.

'And,' he added, 'transferring your business.'

Her head shot round. 'Where to?'

'Columbine's.'

Nature reasserted itself and Bella's lungs gasped for air.

'I'd hand over to you an area in which you could set up shop. I'd allocate you a sum of money with which to construct a replica of a village store. You could make it as chummy and as old-fashioned as you liked. Stock it as you thought fit. Call it by any name of your choosing. Then, I warn you, you'd have to prove yourself. Or else.'

'Reece?' Her voice was husky with emotion, her eyes sparkling with tears of gratitude. 'You would?' He nodded. 'But—but wouldn't you have to put it to the board? Of Columbine's, I mean?'

'It would be my money I'd use to subsidise you. If the venture's successful, then and only then would I ask Strong Nation to consider taking it on board.'

She was silent for so long, he looked at her askance. 'Does the prospect frighten you? Where's your confi-dence gone?' he taunted. 'All that sales talk you levelled at me earlier, about the personal touch, that old and tested technique of dealing person-to-person over the counter?'

'It's—it's just that I can't get over your generosity in making such an offer.'

'You're overwhelmed? Don't be.' He took her hand and with it tapped the top of his own head. 'It's hard, isn't it? Yes, Bella, I'm a hard-headed businessman as you implied just now. This idea has come from that part of my anatomy, not this.' He moved her hand down to his chest, in the region of his heart, pressing her palm against him. 'Yes, I've got one, even though I can see from your expression that you doubt it. But I keep it firmly in its place.'

Especially, Bella thought, where women are concerned. She made to remove her hand from its disturbing contact with his body and he let it go.

'What I'm trying to do,' Bella told him, 'is to visualise Food Fare within the context of the glare and glitter of Columbine's.'

'That's an odd way to describe a supermarket,' was his amused answer, 'but I think I see what you mean. The brilliant lighting, the bright colours. I'd give you a quiet corner. It would be up to you to use whatever means you think appropriate to attract custom. You wouldn't lack the cash, Bella. I'd subsidise you to the hilt.'

'Reece,' those tears welled again, her hand strayed to rest on his bare, hair-sprinkled arm, 'I don't know how to thank you.'

His head turned slowly towards her. 'Don't try. After a few weeks, you might even curse me. It'll be hard work. My standards are high. But I remembered what Jacqueline said about your sales technique, how you apparently persuaded her, so subtly she didn't realise it at the time, to buy much more than she'd originally intended.'

He smiled, and her heart turned over. But, she told herself firmly, there'd been nothing in that underbrowed look he'd given her except the expectation of good business as a result of her 'persuasive' touch.

'After a trial period,' he went on, 'I'd expect sales to justify my investment in you. Regard it,' his eyes narrowed, 'as an experiment, a kind of whim on my part.

OK?' She nodded, so happy she could dance. 'There's a condition.'

His words did not immediately register, but when they did sink in her heart sank with them because she could tell by his tone that the 'condition' he intended to impose was one that she might not want to accept.

'When the shop and the house attached to it becomes mine, where will you live?'

It had not occurred to her that his 'hard-headed' business proposition might make her homeless. Her fingers around her knees grew white with tension.

'M-my father—maybe he'll let me live there.'

'The apartment he's occupying is one-bedroomed. Think again, Bella.'

'I'll just have to rent a place, won't I? Or,' her smile was strained, 'find a nice roomy cardboard box and a quiet part of the street——'

'Quit fooling, Bella.'

'The answer is,' irritably, because he had verbally cornered her and knew it, 'I don't know.' A heavy sigh escaped her. 'I'll have to look through the classified ads for a flat to let, won't I, not too expensive, of course?'

'Which brings us to the salary I'm willing to pay you. And to my condition.'

Salary she hadn't even thought about in her joy at Food Fare's being rescued and offered a new lease of life. The nature of that 'condition' was what she feared most.

'Will you please put me out of my misery?'

He gave a short laugh. 'You talk as if I'm committing you to a term of imprisonment. OK, it's this. My sister Jacqueline's moving out very soon. She and Dick have found a house and she's intending to transfer to it before their marriage to do the necessary decorating, and so on. She told you?' There was a slant to his smile. 'She's been a good little sister and looked after her big brother very well. I need someone to step into her shoes, Bella. I'm offering that job to you.'

Confused, Bella tried to put things into perspective. 'How do you mean?'

'As a housekeeper. Live-in. No strings. You'd occupy her part of the house, quite separate from mine, except for use of kitchen and main living-rooms. It would solve your accommodation problems, and the duties wouldn't be exactly onerous.'

'Would I have to clean and cook and do the washing?' she heard herself ask, quite against the agitated voice of her reason. Don't do it, it was saying, think how often you'd see him, how your lives would intermingle. It would be emotional torture. You might have regarded him in the past as your enemy, but you know very well how you feel about him now. What about after you've lived with him...no, not lived with him, shared his house in an entirely professional capacity...?

'No to the first,' he answered, 'you'd have help with that, and yes to the third and the second. That is, if you can. Cook, I mean.'

'Not exactly *haute cuisine*, but my efforts satisfied my father.'

'OK by me. And generally keep the place tidy,' he added.

Bella was at war with herself. She was being pulled in so many directions she couldn't say a word. At last, she asked, 'So your offer of establishing Food Fare within Columbine's is conditional on my saying yes to being your housekeeper?'

It seemed to take him a long time to answer. Was he at war with himself, too? 'It is. What's wrong?' His tone was jeering now. 'Is it so reprehensible to you to consider moving to the "other side of the town", as I'm reliably informed you used to call it, an area you've had a grudge against since childhood, that you'd even give up the chance of your business's being upgraded?'

If she agreed, it would be a way of avoiding telling him the truth—that working under his authority every day and virtually *living* with him week after week but on an entirely platonic basis might be such a strain on her system that, after a time, she couldn't bear it.

'It would mean living in your house,' she remarked dubiously.

'Of course. Which would no doubt be against your very peculiar set of principles.' He was angry now, the line of his profile hard against the cloud-scattered blue sky. 'Mixing with the so-called wealthy, the moneyed class—you always did have a down on people like the Strangor-Denmans, didn't you? OK,' he sprang up, waiting impatiently for her to release his sweater and pulling it on, 'forget the whole thing.'

He strode off and she made a dive for his arm, finding a bunch of sweater in her fist. 'Reece, I didn't say that. It's just that—oh, you wouldn't understand.' At last he halted, deliberately disengaging her fingers from his clothing. She looked up at him, eyes wide and appealing. 'I agree, to your offer and your condition.'

'Because you've got no other option?' he asked coldly. 'As I said, forget it.' He turned to go, but she caught at his hand this time, gripping it with both of hers like someone desperately grasping a rising rope from a rescuing helicopter.

'What else, Reece, would you have me base my acceptance on? Why else does *anyone*, apart from the very lucky ones who love their calling, accept *any* job, except through necessity?' And except a fool like me who's fallen in love with her future boss.

His expression was so inscrutable, she shook his arm. 'I've given you my answer, Reece. It's yes. Please,' she added, attempting a smile, head on one side.

There was an answering glimmer in his eyes, but it soon faded. They reached the car and he was politeness itself as he showed her into the passenger seat. His manner remained cool as he stared through the windscreen, making no attempt to start the engine.

'Now, I'm going to shock you to your class-conscious, inverted-snobbery-bound roots. How about this for a salary, for the combined position of housekeeper to me, and manager of the over-the-counter sales section of Columbine's?' He named a figure that totally deprived her of breath.

Having recovered it with difficulty, she exclaimed, 'But—but I'm not worth that!'

'You aren't?' His granite-hard eyes sought hers. 'You damned well will be, when I've finished with you. Well, do you accept, or do you want to bargain with me?' He smiled like a man spoiling for a fight, bunching his fists pugilistically. 'You should, if you know your own worth. Come on, persuade me to raise it.' He smiled again, thrusting out his jaw. 'I'll take you on. It'll be a pleasure,' his gaze skimmed over her, 'an erotic pleasure.'

Colouring deeply at the suggestion of intimacy implicit in his look, she declared, 'Now who's bringing emotion into a business discussion?'

'"Emotion", lady,' he answered, eyes hooded, 'was the last thing I had in mind at that moment.'

Of course it was, she told herself angrily. What would a night spent with one of the Bella Harrisons of this world be for a man like Reece Denman but a casual, passing fling with no emotional involvement whatsoever? Especially with someone like the beautiful Marguerite Hunter-Parkes waiting in the wings to sweep on stage and take her place beside him as the only real and lasting passion in his life?

'The trouble with your contention,' she remarked, dragging her thoughts and the conversation back on to safer lines, 'that I should know my own value by now is that after working for so many years for a loving father, who's praised me on every possible occasion, I just don't know it. How could I?'

'In the great big world of commerce, you mean? In competition with others? OK,' he started the car and they exited from the Duke's Park through the great triumphal arch, 'so now you're going to get your chance. The housekeeping job becomes vacant in seven days' time. I'll see my lawyer about starting the process of buying you out. You should instruct a solicitor, too. I'll speak to your father and we'll all get together and discuss a price for the premises. Apart from bricks and mortar, I imagine it has little other value.'

'There's the goodwill,' Bella retaliated fiercely. 'Never forget that. I'll talk all my customers into patronising my new store.'

Reece laughed, head back, eyes still on the road. 'That's my Bella Harrison. Fight every inch of the way, Isabella, and you'll convince me I've done the right thing, businesswise, in placing my trust in you.' His goading smile flicked her face as they drew to a stop at traffic-lights.

'If you're referring to my character as regards my job as your housekeeper,' she hit back, 'if I don't have your trust, then we might as well end it here and now.'

He turned sleepy eyes towards her. 'End it, Bella, when it's hardly begun?' The lights changed and they moved on.

Pulling up outside the shop, he stopped her, his hand covering hers. 'Feel free to come to my house any time to look at the rooms you're going to occupy. I'll get things moving. Agreed?'

She nodded and his hand gripped hers in a binding clasp. 'To our future relationship.'

'Strictly business, no strings.' She flashed a smile. 'Your words, Mr Denman. On that basis—agreed.'

'Arm's length from the word go, Miss Harrison,' he conceded. What worried Bella most at that moment was the glint in his eye.

CHAPTER EIGHT

WHEN Bella telephoned her father, it was Maddy Langridge who answered. Since it was evening, when even a semi-retired nurse would have been expected to be at home, Bella was immediately alarmed.

'Is my father ill, Maddy?' she asked anxiously.

Maddy's laugh was reassuring. 'He's fine, dear. I'm just keeping him company for a while. I'll put him on to you.'

'Dad? I just have to tell you. Very soon now, I'll be working under the same roof as you again.'

It all came pouring out, Reece's offer to purchase Food Fare, transferring the business to Columbine's, his request to her to become his housekeeper in return for a place to live.

'Was I right to accept, Dad?' she asked at last. 'And since you've still got a financial interest in the business, do you agree to the sale?'

'You were right, lass, and I accept. But have you given it some thought, Bella? It's two jobs he's expecting you to do. I know you're young, but even youth has its breaking-point if it's expected to carry too many burdens.'

Bella laughed. 'You make me sound as if I were an overladen mule climbing a mountain!' she exclaimed. 'I'll love the challenge.'

'And the housekeeping?' He paused as if a thought had struck him. 'You'd be alone in the house, lass, with a very—using my old-fashioned words—eligible young bachelor. Have you considered that point of view?'

'In other words, am I worried about my reputation?' She laughed again. 'No, I'm not. From what I hear, I've been dubbed "hot property", if you know what I mean, by some villagers for having two boyfriends. I doubt if having a third quite falsely added to the list by scandal-mongers would do me much harm. Anyway, it's well known who Reece Denman's real lady-friend is. He'd hardly stoop to having even a clandestine affair with a lowly shop assistant like me!'

'Bella!' She had angered her father. 'Stop saying such things, and stop denigrating yourself, even in fun. You're an intelligent and very attractive young lady, with lots of excellent ideas. But when you get on your "class-conscious" soap box, dear, you annoy me very much.'

Maddy's laugh rang out in the background.

'Sorry,' Bella answered contritely. 'But when I need a reference for another job one day, I'll give your name! You wouldn't be prejudiced, of course?'

'Certainly not,' her father answered, then proceeded to congratulate her and discuss the terms of the purchase of the business.

When Bella rang Jacqueline to tell her about the changes which were about to take place in her life, her friend gave a whoop of delight.

'I knew my brother would turn up trumps,' she cried. 'And to ask you to move in here and take over what I do for him—that was a master stroke. He obviously knows a good thing when he sees one. Not that you're a "thing", dear,' she added, laughing. 'But I warn you, Bella, he's not always easy to get on with, especially when he's got business on his mind, which is nearly every minute of the day. Still want to accept his offer?'

'I'd lose so much if I turned it down, Jacqueline. Anyway, unlike you because you're his sister, I can always give in my notice,' she joked.

'Come and look over the place any time you like,' Jacqueline invited. 'How about tomorrow?'

So, the following evening, after Food Fare closed, Jacqueline answered her knock and joyfully welcomed her. She put a finger to her lips. 'The tiger's in his den. He's in a fine old tail-swinging mood. I warn you, when he's like that, stay clear. Now,' she led the way to the left of the entrance hall and flung open her living-room door, 'as you know by now, my rooms are this way. Reece's are back there.' She indicated the area to the right of the main entrance. 'Up the stairs and over these rooms, there's my bedroom and bathroom. Let's wander. Pretend it's all yours. Which it will be in a few days' time.'

Having followed in a daze wherever her friend led, Bella sank into the feather-soft cushions of a deep chair back in Jacqueline's small and cosy living-room and shook her head. 'I just can't believe that all this is going to be mine. I won't want to change a thing.'

'How about a nice cup of tea,' Jacqueline said, and invited Bella to join her in the kitchen which, she explained, she shared with her brother, along with the main living-room. 'Ah,' she remarked, turning at the sound in the doorway, 'I thought the rattle of crockery might entice the wild animal from his lair. Could you do with a cup, dear brother, to soothe your "savage breast"?'

'I could, thanks.' Arms folded, his tall, commanding figure framed by the doorway, Reece looked from one to the other as Jacqueline assembled the necessary crockery. She made a sisterly face while waiting for him to move aside and swept out, saying 'Won't be long' to Bella and carrying the tray across to her own part of the house. All the while, the kettle came to the boil, filling the difficult silence.

'Making yourself at home, I see,' Reece commented at last, quirking an eyebrow.

Bridling at the implied sarcasm, she parried tartly, gazing up at him, 'Do you object? Would you have preferred me to stand to attention the moment the master of the house, and my future boss, made his appearance? Because if so, you've backed the wrong person for the job.'

He moved towards her, eyelids lowered, mouth curved in an enigmatic smile. 'Oh, no, Miss Harrison,' he said, voice misleadingly soft, 'I only bet on certainties. The gamble I'm taking with you won't fail. You fit the specification like a made-to-measure glove.'

He proceeded to do another lightning survey of her face and figure.

'Easy on the eye, too,' he went on, 'which is a bonus. Just great for a man to come home to. But,' before she could protest indignantly at his male chauvinism, he reached out and pulled her by her hands from the breakfast bar stool, 'if, in the weeks to come, you persist in dragging class divisions into every aspect and nuance of our future relationshp, I'll——' his strong arms forced her closer and he put his whispering lips to her ear, sending an alarming series of tingles through the nerves of her neck and spine '—I'll put you across my knee and spank you until you yell for mercy. Get it?'

The kettle came frantically to the boil and clicked itself off, delivering a timely warning only seconds before Jacqueline swept back into the kitchen. She looked askance at her brother as he pushed his hands into his pockets, then at her friend as she turned her hectic flush towards the window.

Reece strolled into Jacqueline's room, lifted his tea from the tray and took it with him, both to Bella's relief and disappointment. At the door, however, he paused.

'When you've finished inspecting your new domain, Bella,' he remarked, 'I'd like a word with you in my study.'

His manner said 'strictly business', and so did his eyes. Jacqueline stared comically after him, then shook her head. 'There are times when I could *bash* my brother. When I'm married, if Dick ever comes the heavy tycoon with me like my brother does to you——'

'But there's the difference,' Bella broke in. 'You'll be Dick's wife, whereas I'm only going to be Reece's employee.'

'All the same, there are ways and ways,' she muttered darkly, 'if you get my meaning.'

Bella helped Jacqueline wash the dishes, then stood outside the door to Reece's study, forefinger curved to knock. In that moment of hesitation, the door was pulled open.

'What kept you?' came the sardonic query. 'You must have stood outside for a full half-minute.'

'I didn't know whether to knock or walk in,' Bella returned quite truthfully as Reece seated himself, 'in case you accused me of introducing class divisions into——'

'OK, so sit,' he hissed, brows thunderously low over cool blue eyes, 'before I come round the desk and use these,' he held up his hands, 'to *make* you.'

Bella complied, mouth curving, eyes bright, waiting for him to speak.

He glanced down at a folder on his desk, clasped his hands and looked at her. 'I've had a long talk with your father. He's delighted at my proposition, which he's no doubt told you. He made two conditions. One, that I don't work you too hard. Two, that I take good care of you. You're all he's got, he says.'

'Doesn't he realise,' Bella replied worriedly, 'that you'll be my employer, not my keeper? I mean,' she hurriedly corrected herself, 'guardian.'

That eyebrow quirked again. '"Keeper", I think, is the word you really meant to use. We'll agree days off, hours you'll be expected to be on duty.'

'Visits of friends,' she put in pointedly. 'Of both sexes.'

'Which is where "keeper" comes in, doesn't it? For "friends" read "boyfriends". Yes?'

'No. I mean, well, maybe.' He continued to look at her. 'Well?' she asked. 'Or, as your housekeeper, will I have to live the life of a nun? Because if so...'

She knew she had gone too far by the thunder in his eyes. He lifted a sheet of paper. 'These are the two contracts I wish you to sign. One concerns your employment under my auspices at Columbine's. And this covers your job as my housekeeper. The terms of both are, in my view and I hope in yours, reasonable. This contains a clause which states that in the event of your entertaining any male in your room overnight in my house,' his eyes grew hard, 'this contract will terminate forthwith.'

Furious, Bella jumped up, leaning forward and resting her hands on the desk. 'You can *keep* your job, *Mr* Denman. I think you're despicable, inserting such a clause in a contract you're expecting *me* to sign.'

Coldly, he rose, closing the folder. 'Thanks for your interest in my offer, Miss Harrison. I can see no reason for carrying on this discussion.'

Unable to believe her ears, Bella made for the door, slamming it behind her. Jacqueline rushed out to meet her.

'What goes on, for heaven's sake?' she asked, seeing Bella's tears. 'Now what's that brother of mine said to you?'

'It's what he expected me to s-sign,' Bella told her, trying to scrub her damp cheeks. 'Implying that I sleep around, th-that I'm in the habit of entertaining men——'

'Oh, no,' Jacqueline moaned. 'Hey, Reece,' she peered round the door of his study, 'you've got to come out here and pick up the pieces. Don't you know how *on the level* Bella is where men are concerned?'

Reece appeared at the door, seeing Bella's distress.

'It's all right,' Bella said, her voice muffled by her handkerchief, 'he's only going by the rumours he's heard about me, and listening to that *wonderful* friend of his, Malcolm Haddern. He believes them, he actually *believes* them! Well, he can keep his job. Bye, Jacqueline. See you some time.'

'Bella!' She had reached the door when her name rang out. It was in a tone she couldn't ignore.

Slowly she turned, her angry tears subsiding. Jacqueline had diplomatically vanished. 'Yes?'

Reece walked over to her, tipping her chin with strong fingers. 'Shall we start again?' His arm around her shoulder impelled her back into his study.

Returning to his seat, he pushed the contracts to her side of the desk. 'Read them, Bella. There's no machiavellian small print. They're honest and straight-forward agreements. This,' he indicated the topmost one, 'relates to your employment by me at Columbine's under the auspices of Strong Nation Holdings of which I'm chief executive. Any financial shortcomings or failure of the business you are undertaking to run will be borne by me.'

Bella nodded. 'It won't fail, I promise.'

Reece smiled but made no comment. 'Will you read it?'

This Bella did, a glow of happiness spreading through her at the chance Reece Denman was giving her. She signed her name, and watched as he added his.

'Thanks, Reece,' she smiled at him warmly, 'from the bottom of my heart.'

His smile back was unreadable, but his reply was only too understandable. 'I never,' he said cryptically, 'bring that organ of the body into my business deals.' Keep your head where our future relations are concerned, it said, and keep out of my private affairs.

Let that be a lesson to you, she instructed herself fiercely.

'Now.' He took away the first contract and pushed the second towards her. 'This deals with your employment as my housekeeper.' She read this, too, and he did not miss her hesitation. He came round the desk to stand beside her. 'That clause stays in, Bella.' The tone was a warning.

'But I——' But I'd never invite any man to stay with me overnight if I didn't love him, she had been going to say. What was the use? He wouldn't have believed her. Anyway, if that was so, and it was, then that clause could never be invoked, could it? With a small sigh, she signed.

As he added his name, he commented, 'If it deprives you of the freedom you've been enjoying in your own home, then that's just too bad.'

'What do you——?' She saw his chiselled profile and realised that he had misinterpreted her sigh. She compressed her lips. She didn't want to quarrel with him again.

'OK, the deed is done.' He looked up and his smile swept a warm swirl of happiness around her heart. 'A good deed, we hope. Shake on it.' His hand came out across the desk and Bella's hand was lost in it. For a few seconds their eyes held and she wished fervently that she were a mind-reader and could interpret Reece's thoughts. Hers, she was certain, were only too plain to see as a shock shot up her arm at the strength and firmness of his grip.

To her relief, the moment passed. He shuffled the papers together, returned to his seat and pushed them back into the folder. It bore the name 'Isabella Harrison'. Which surely showed just how he regarded her—as part of the purely business side of his life, an employee, a name to be filed away, nothing more.

'But, Bella,' Jimmy remonstrated as he walked with her across the fields, his dog nosing out all her favourite smells, 'you always had such a down on that side of the town,' his nod indicated the area of which he was speaking, 'especially the Strangor-Denmans. What possessed you to agree to go and work over there? Not just work there, but *live* there?'

He made her feel terrible, as though she were letting him and Vernon and all her friends down, too. How could she tell him that love knew no barriers? He'd call it corny and sentimental.

'That was a long time ago,' she tried to explain. 'And how could it have been just the Strangor-Denmans when Jacqueline was—still is, really—my best friend? Maybe,' she frowned, 'it was just a straightforward question of the "haves" versus the "have nots", and I felt, rightly or wrongly, that my parents and I belonged to the "have nots".'

Jimmy didn't seem convinced.

'This was the only way,' she insisted, 'to save the business—Food Fare, I mean. Reece Denman finally agreed to help, and in a way I couldn't possibly refuse, not only for my sake but Dad's.' She explained Reece's idea about her opening an old-fashioned shop within Columbine's. 'He's giving me a chance I couldn't even have dreamed up.'

'Right. But did you have to go and accept the job of waiting on Reece Denman hand and foot?'

'Jimmy,' she said gently as they paused by the stile, 'when the shop finally shuts and Reece closes down the whole place, I'd be homeless. Where would I live?'

'We've got a spare room,' he said doggedly. 'My mum would be only too pleased to have you there and look after you.'

The warning light was flashing. She would have to tread very carefully so as not to hurt Jimmy's feelings, nor to give him any encouragement.

'It's great of you to say that,' she squeezed his arm, 'but—well, I hope you won't misunderstand me and think me mercenary when I say that the salary that goes with both jobs is so good I'd be an idiot to refuse.'

After staring for a while into the distance, his shrug, resigned as it was, finally told her that he was becoming reconciled. He called to his dog, and they turned for home.

'What about Polly?' he asked. 'Will she lose her job?'

'No. She's coming with me as my assistant. She'll be paid much more. Reece agreed. She's very pleased.'

His grunt revealed that he was glad she hadn't forgotten the hard-working young woman who had stayed at her side through the difficult weeks that were now behind them.

The following days passed in a whirl, the sale of the business and the house to Reece progressing smoothly. Bella had put up notices informing her customers that the shop wasn't really closing, it was being transferred.

Edgar spent some time going through his few possessions that still remained in the house, and told Bella that any furniture that was left would be for her to keep or dispose of as she liked.

Jacqueline helped her pack crockery and glassware to take for a jumble sale collection, but when it came to either giving away or packing up her own things no one could help. It was, Bella told her friend, for her to face on her own.

The last evening was a Saturday and Jacqueline left Bella's house early in order to do her own packing so that Bella could move into her rooms. Bella was pushing the final articles into an overstretched suitcase, when she became aware of the emptiness and the silence all around her.

It was so still she could almost hear her own heart beating. Voices tuned in from the past, her mother calling to her to come to breakfast, chiding Edgar for not removing his muddy shoes after coming in from the garden, her father laughing as he calmed his wife with a kiss, then greeting his daughter with a cheerful 'good morning'.

Bella covered her ears, then her face, trying in vain to hold back the tears. All the years she had spent there came crowding in on her, her happy childhood, her noisy schooldays, her fiery adolescence, and she knew that she would be leaving a very large part of herself behind.

A floorboard creaked. She thought it was her father calling in for a farewell visit, until an arm came round her impelling her backwards into a powerful, yet strangely comforting embrace, against an iron-hard chest that supported the back of her resting head, a breeze-clean handkerchief being pushed into her hand.

'I'm s-sorry,' she sobbed, wiping her tears, 'but I suddenly remembered——'

'Voices from the past? Loving memories haunting you?' Reece asked. She nodded against him and he turned her gently. 'They're alive, Bella, those memories.' She had never guessed that he could be so sensitive, so understanding. 'You won't leave them behind, you'll take them with you. All through your life. Some people have sad ones to their dying day. But aren't you the lucky one?' He tipped her face, searching her eyes. 'Yours will be happy.'

He took the handkerchief and stroked her cheeks dry.

'W-what do you know of unhappy m-memories?' she queried, calming down. 'You've never wanted for money, or anything, have you? You and Jacqueline, you both only had to ask and you were given. Jacqueline told me.'

'That's my girl,' he said, his smile intense but fleeting, 'fighting back.' His glance grew guarded and he released her. 'Money doesn't buy everything.'

'That's true.' She pushed with her foot at the worn carpet pile, noting how the pattern had almost disappeared. Then her head lifted defiantly. 'In buying this place and offering me a job—two jobs—you haven't bought me.'

'Agreed.' He gave a cut-off laugh. 'The Isabella Harrison, proud ship that she is, sets off on her voyage to a new life, all guns blazing.' His smile faded and he looked around. 'I came to see if there was anything I could do to help.'

She shook her head. 'Thanks, but I was just leaving.'

He nodded. 'Bleak, isn't it? I'm not surprised it was beginning to get to you. These the keys? OK, I'll take charge of them.'

'They're yours now, anyway.'

'Shush.' His finger rested momentarily on her lips. 'No bitterness, no regrets. My sister's bedroom's ready and waiting. She'll finish the other rooms tomorrow.'

As they reached his car, Bella gave one last glance back, then got into the passenger seat and looked resolutely towards the future.

Reece drew up outside Windham House. 'Look on it, Bella, as your home. Will you try to do that for me?'

'Why?' she said defensively. 'I'm your new employee now, not your new w-w——' The word stuck in her throat. Had she spoken it her voice would have trembled

and that would have told him at once of her vulnerability where he was concerned.

'Why?' he answered, ignoring her hesitation. 'Because it would make life so much easier for both of us.
In the circumstances, we can't live in a permanent state
of semi-warfare.'

He was right, as usual. She sighed, and whispered,
'I'll try.'

His hand covered hers. 'Come on in.' In the hall he
turned to face her and smiled, holding out his hand. She
put hers into it and once again the shock of the contact
sent an alarming tingle around her nervous system.

'Welcome, Isabella Harrison, to the Strangor-Denman
residence,' he said. 'Whether you like it or not, Bella,
you've made it to the other side of the town.'

Bella studied the list which Jacqueline had pinned to the
kitchen notice-board. 'Times when the tiger in his den
likes to be fed:' Then in brackets, 'Except Sundays, when
he just sits and roars for his feed.'

Thank goodness it's Sunday, Bella thought, amused
by her friend's sisterly instructions. Then she frowned.
If Reece really did expect instant meals when it should
have been her own day of relaxation too, her life was
going to be one long hassle. 'Even youth,' her father
had said, 'has its breaking-point.' Maybe he'd been right
after all?

'Don't believe a word she says,' commented a voice
from the doorway. 'My sibling's little joke.' He leant
sideways, arms folded, against the doorframe, short-
sleeved navy mesh shirt pushed into the waistband of
his faded jeans, dark hair ruffled as though roughly dried
after a shower.

He looked vital and tough and alarmingly attractive,
and Bella had to look away to hide the admiration in
her eyes. This was a Reece Denman she'd never

encountered before. How, she asked herself desperately, was she going to cope for all the time she worked for him with all the feelings of longing he was arousing within her? And this was just her first morning in the job!

'You aren't, are you?' she asked anxiously. 'A finger-drummer on the table if your meals aren't served exactly on time? Because if you are, I'll——'

'Leave?' His eyes narrowed.

'The other way, probably. It's more likely I'll be fired! My pace wouldn't be your pace, and you'll get impatient and show me the door.'

'Take it easy, Miss Harrison.' He spoke softly, insinuatingly, his eyes doing a kind of routine inspection of her figure. 'A girl with your—er—assets would have to drive a man a hell of a way up the wall before he unfurled his claws and said, "Out."' His smile was full of irony. 'What's wrong now? The feminist in you shrieking blue murder at my remarks? They're meant as compliments.' He lifted himself upright, advancing into the room. "That's the trouble with women today. They seem to regard a man's tributes to their beauty and sexual attractiveness as insults.'

He looked her over again, but this time with a frown. His fingers flicked the collar of her neat white blouse, then moved to rest for a fleeting second on her hip, touching the fabric of her plain black skirt. 'What's this? A kind of uniform? For God's sake, this is Sunday. Relax, Bella. Loosen up. Anyway, what are you playing at? Parlour maid to my master of the house?'

'It's my first day. I didn't know what to wear.'

His eyes slitted. 'I could tell you, but I won't.' He made for the fridge, took out some milk and straightened to face her. 'Rule number one. Sundays, I feed myself. OK? Breakfast in here. Sometimes, I go out to lunch. Evening time, I raid the freezer, cook whatever, and carry it where I'm working. Or watching television.' He lifted a shoulder. 'Entertaining... whoever. You're with me?'

She nodded, but wished she weren't. His words had reminded her of her place, as his employee, not his companion. For that, he turned to others, women, and one woman in particular. Well, I'll have to take it, she lectured herself. Like it or not, he had female friends.

'Am I to understand,' her chin lifted, 'that Sunday is my day off, too?'

He helped himself to cereal, pouring milk over it. 'Anything wrong with that? Since it's the only day you, like me, will be free of any obligations workwise, it seems like a good idea.'

'Thanks. And,' she moistened her lips, 'if I want—friends in, in my part of the house, I mean, I hope you won't object?'

'Friends being male? No objection, provided the proviso in our agreement is adhered to.'

She slammed the cupboard door and he looked up. '*Thank* you,' she answered between her teeth.

He opened the Sunday paper, shedding layers on to the floor, putting aside the news section and colour magazine and propping up the financial pages in front of him.

He seemed to become aware of her movements. 'Where are you going?'

She stood at the door holding her tray filled with her own breakfast dishes. 'To my living-room.'

'Why? What's wrong with here? Inverted snobbery, is it? Beneath Isabella Harrison's dignity to eat in the kitchen, even one as pleasant as this?'

Careful, she cautioned herself, it's your first day, and he is, after all, your employer. 'It's my day off, too, I think you said?'

He switched off abruptly and gave all his attention to his reading matter.

She was reclining luxuriously on Jacqueline's sofa reading a paperback, feet bare, trouser-legs rucked up and showing her calves and ankles, when the door opened. Her round-necked pink T-shirt had twisted, revealing a smooth white shoulder, her hair lay tumbled over the padded arm beneath her head. Unable to decipher her employer's expression, she asked, 'Am I doing something wrong? You told me to relax, so I'm taking you at your word. If there's anything you want——' She made to rise but his uplifted hand stopped her.

He strolled across to drop on the other, larger sofa and rested his head on uplifted hands, stretching out his legs, eyes steadily on her. She grew pink under his scrutiny.

'If I'm not behaving like your idea of a housekeeper,' she said with a touch of acid, 'if you'll outline your particular requirements I'll do my best to oblige.'

He gave a short bark of a laugh. 'I can see that you'll certainly add more colour, not to mention spice, to my life.' He rose and stood, hands in pockets, looking down at her. 'My reason for trespassing on your time and territory was because I'd like you to come with me to the store this morning.'

'To Columbine's? But why?' She swung her legs into a sitting position. 'I don't start until tomorrow, do I?'

'And today's your day off. All the same, I'd like to show you round outside shopping hours, discuss various matters connected with the corner you're going to occupy.'

It was an order in disguise, Bella told herself, one she couldn't have refused even if she'd wanted to.

'Also,' he went on, 'I'm going north tomorrow for a few days. I'm paying unannounced visits to our various stores in Yorkshire and Scotland.'

'Which means I'll be on my own? With just myself to look after, I mean?'

'Without having to worry about the boss's welfare, yes,' he said with a smile. 'And if you continue to look as if you'd licked the cream jug dry at the thought of my absence from the house,' he crouched down, 'I'll personally throttle you with these.' He held up his hands, then settled them around her neck. She could not prevent herself from shivering as those hands enfolded her throat.

Their eyes clashed and locked and, although she fought him fiercely, in the battle he was indisputably the winner. The light of surrender must have been in her eyes since he urged her towards him and claimed her lips, parting them until they trembled under the exploring impact of his.

'That's what you get,' he said, releasing her at last and pocketing his hands as he straightened, 'for looking at me like that.'

'No, I didn't,' she protested heatedly, 'not in any special way.'

'No?' His smile was sardonic, unbelieving. He moved his head, indicating the door. 'Join me in three minutes flat. A second late, and you're fired. OK?'

'No employer,' she threw after him, 'can sack his employee on her day off.'

'Just try me,' he shot at her, swinging round, and she could not judge from his expression whether or not she had truly angered him.

Bella changed into smarter trousers, ran a comb through her hair and ran downstairs to join him. Traffic was light on the roads as they drove to the store. Reece parked in a privileged place which bore his name and Bella was aware of a tiny twist of emotion, not of resentment any more, but of sheer, if inexplicable, pride.

He used his keys and stood back to allow her to pass into the building. It was curious entering a great supermarket which was totally empty of human beings, for whom the place existed anyway. The silent shelves held themselves aloof, as if challenging: Touch us if you dare.

Something in her recoiled at the impersonality of the displays, recognising many of the brands that she herself had stocked in a shop that had had so much more warmth and familiarity about it than this place. Well, it would be her job, soon, to recreate Harrison's Food Fare within these slightly overpowering walls.

Bella followed where Reece went, her senses alert, taking in the atmosphere without the intrusion of the crowds coming between herself and the store's essence. She could see the subtlety with which the products had been displayed, feel the pulling power of colour and lighting.

'How does it strike you?' he asked, looking round, hands in pockets.

'They're saying,' she answered thoughtfully, lifting her hand and indicating the immediate environment, 'buy me because I want your money, because my owners want to make a profit, not because you need me, nor because I'm essential to you in the way you run your home, feed your family.'

'An astute, very Bella-like remark. OK, so it's like a theatre set.'

'The colours draw you.'

'Right. In the lay-out as a whole, the designers and marketing men will tell you, there's a market atmosphere encouraging people to walk all over the place and then buy on impulse.'

'So psychology comes into it,' she remarked, wrinkling her nose.

He smiled satirically. 'So it does! What's wrong with that?' He turned, pointing to the main entrance. 'There's the profit motive operating right at the start of the family shopping expedition. At the back,' he swung round, 'food is retained to entice people into buying unintended extras. Are you with me?' He glanced down at her. 'You are, and you wish you weren't, hm?'

'Oh, I don't mind being with you at all, Reece...' She realised by his broad smile that she had misunderstood him, to his amusement and her own chagrin. 'Yes, I get it,' she answered, colouring. 'Replace my word "psychology" with "trickery".'

His expression hardened and he walked on, leaving her to catch him up. 'I'm sorry if I annoyed you,' she said, 'but I was only saying what I thought. It'll probably happen a lot in our future dealings. If you don't like my bluntness, which is second nature to me——'

He stopped and looked down at her. 'Do you really think I've known Isabella Harrison for all these years without also knowing her personality?'

'But in the past you hardly spoke to me.'

'The eyes and the perception can often tell you as much, if not more about a person than hours of talking and discussion.' He stopped in a corner of the store. 'Here is where you'll be.'

'It's basic, isn't it?' she commented with a frown.

The space he indicated covered about the same area as her father's shop. It already contained a certain number of fixtures, the fittings, such as they were, being far more modern than those she had been used to. She glanced over her shoulder at the rest of the store, then looked back at the area with dismay.

'It's so tucked away, people won't know I'm here. How will I get custom? How can I entice shoppers from the main store into this small space?'

'One, it's larger than you think. Two, that's your problem, pal.'

His sudden lapse into the 'brother of Jacqueline' role made her heart beat faster.

'It's all yours,' he went on. 'Any help you need with measurements and so on, just let me know. Cheer up,

Isabella,' he said softly, tipping her chin—no one but he, she thought abstractedly, said her name in that special way. 'Imagine you're back in Food Fare. Take it from there.' He took her left hand in his right. 'It's up to you to prove yourself, Bella. It won't be easy, but I know you've got the fighting spirit to put this area of the store on the map.'

Her eyes were wide with apprehension as she raised them to his. 'Do you honestly think I'll succeed?' She saw his gaze flicker and translated it as doubt. 'You don't,' she said dully, removing her hand from his.

'So prove me wrong.'

Her head lifted proudly. 'I will, Mr Denman, even if it kills me.'

'You'll live,' he commented, leading the way out.

CHAPTER NINE

'JIMMY, will you help me? With the design of the space I've been allocated in Columbine's, I mean? You know, décor, colour choice, that sort of thing.'

Lying full-length on her side on the rectangle of lilac-coloured carpeting immediately beneath the matching two-seater sofa in her little living-room, telephone to her ear, Bella waited hopefully for Jimmy's answer.

He was slow to give it, plainly taken aback by her request. 'I'm not qualified, Bella,' he said at last. 'My line's——'

'I know what your job is, Jimmy. I also know you're gifted artistically. I've got a collection of the sketches you've made of me and my dad in the past. And the flowers you've drawn on some of our walks.'

'That doesn't mean I could design you a shop.'

'*Please*, Jimmy, would you have a try? I could get anyone I wanted—money no object—but I'd rather have you——'

Work with me, she'd been going to add, but a sound at the entrance made her head turn. 'Just a minute,' she said into the telephone, then covered it with her palm. 'Yes?' she asked Reece. 'Did you want me?'

There was a pause while cold eyes did a raking survey of her stretched-out figure. She let out an irritated breath. So he was choosing to misunderstand her, deliberately translating her expression 'want', both to himself and to Jimmy, into a statement with intimate undertones.

130

'Later.' He turned to go. 'I'd hate to interrupt your whisper of loving words and phrases in your boyfriend's ear.' The door clicked shut.

Bella sighed again. 'Sorry, Jimmy,' she said, then repeated her plea for his assistance in her new venture. 'And do you think Vernon would be willing to install the shelving and cabinets? Yes, I know what *his* job is, too, but I also know that he's a gifted handyman type. I've seen all those fitments he's put in for your parents at your house.'

'OK,' Jimmy capitulated, 'I'll do what I can for you. I'll ask Vernon, too.'

'The—er—remuneration will be good,' she added persuasively. Jimmy laughed and said he'd be in touch.

Bella scrambled up and went to find Reece. He was where she had thought he would be, in his office along the hallway. His eyes conveyed no 'welcome' message. This, Bella thought, was business.

'The area I've given you within Columbine's,' he said, without preamble, swinging slowly in his office chair, and indicating that she could sit or stand as she wished, 'will remain untouched until you occupy it. What I'm saying is,' he waited, leaning forward, hands clasped on the desk and watching her as she removed the stack of papers from the chair opposite him, then occupied it, 'that your employment as the manager of the family shop within the larger store begins tomorrow whether or not you're actually on the premises. You know the ropes regarding ordering stock, arranging for the fittings you need——'

'Could I interrupt and ask you something?' He nodded, eyes cool and impartial. 'I was talking to Jimmy Canford just now and no,' she declared, seeing his cynical look, 'it wasn't to tell him I love him because I don't.'

Oh, heavens, she thought, seeing his expression harden, now he's convinced I'm having a heartless, loveless affair with my boyfriend.

'I was asking him,' she went on, 'if he and his brother Vernon would like to take on the design and construction of the display stands and the painting for me, and so on. I hope you don't mind.'

He paused, staring at his clasped hands. 'There's no need to employ amateurs. You can have the best. I told you I'd bear the expense.'

'I know, but you see,' she looked at her hands, 'first, I never like to spend money unnecessarily——'

'What a fantastic wife you'll make one day for some lucky man.'

It was the cynicism in his tone that annoyed her. 'Now who's bringing personalities into this discussion?'

He patted the air, calming her down, but his eyes stayed cynical.

'Thanks, anyway,' Bella continued, 'for allowing me an unlimited budget for getting the project off the ground, but I felt that someone like Jimmy and Vernon would know—well, what ordinary, everyday customers might like.'

'I get it,' he rasped. 'In your eyes, the Canfords are the "good guys", in your *class*.'

Bella bristled. 'I hadn't thought of it that way, but yes, if you like. If—if you want a fight,' to her horror she heard herself burst out, 'you can have it.'

He would never know how near the tears came to filling her eyes. Wouldn't they ever be able to agree on anything? Would they be fighting each other to the end of their lives? Not, she realistically pointed out to herself, that they'd know each other that long.

To her surprise and immense relief he laughed, plainly enjoying the prospect she offered him.

'Reece?' she asked from the doorway. He looked up from the papers he had drawn towards him. 'How can we be sure you aren't wasting your money? I mean, how do we know this idea will succeed?'

'You can stop worrying, Isabella,' he drawled, leaning back and plainly appreciating her attractions. 'You know Bruce Hunter-Parkes of Hunter-Parkes Associates?'

'The market research man? Father of your——?' Lady-friend, she just prevented herself from saying.

He must have known, but he gave no sign. 'I employed his marketing team to do a survey. The answer they came up with was a definite yes. Satisfied?'

She nodded. 'I should have known you were too canny a businessman to take a chance like that without first testing the waters.'

'I took a chance on you, didn't I?' he countered, lids half lowered. 'Employing you on this venture, not to mention as my housekeeper, without first *testing the waters*?'

His meaning was only too clear, but she blurted out, 'I don't know what you mean.'

'No?' He got to his feet. 'Want a demonstration?'

Bella fled.

Reece was away longer than Bella had expected. Although she missed his vital presence in the house, and at night was over-conscious of its size and her own vulnerability where security was concerned, in one sense she was glad.

It enabled her, with Jimmy's and Vernon's willing help, to work on her little shop-within-a-shop evening after evening without having to hurry back and prepare meals for Reece.

'I want it to be as much like Food Fare as we can possibly make it,' she pronounced, 'but with modern materials which can be scrubbed and polished and kept squeaky clean to please the food inspectors.'

Which, by the time Reece was due home, was, she felt, exactly what she and the two brothers had finally achieved. The stock she had ordered was ready to be unpacked and put into place, the frozen food cabinets scoured and ready to be switched on, the lighting adequate and not too bright, the better to go with the 'village store' image she had striven so hard to create.

'When's the boss coming home?' Vernon asked, rolling down his sleeves and peering round the tall screens which had hidden their 'work of art', as he called it, from public scrutiny before it was ready. 'Tomorrow, I think you said? So,' pulling on his sweater, 'let's go out and celebrate. Drinks on me. OK?'

'Well, I——' Bella hesitated. She was tired, but Jimmy was looking at her so beseechingly, she nodded.

Then she looked at Vernon. 'Er—a threesome doesn't usually work,' she remarked with affected casualness. 'Couldn't you ask Mary to join us?'

Vernon's cheeks turned pink. 'Might. Maybe.' His smile was a touch sheepish. 'If it's OK with you, Bella?'

That was, Bella considered, as good as saying, I hope you don't mind but I like her a lot. He peeled off his overall and rolled it into a bundle, pushing it under his arm.

'You take Bella,' he told his brother, 'and I'll get Mary.'

After a few drinks at the Rising Sun, Bella asked them back to the house. After leading the way to her own living-room, she stood looking down at their sprawling figures. 'I think,' she said, 'you've all imbibed too freely in celebration of our achievement.'

Vernon laughed, then hiccupped.

'Tea all round, I think,' Bella pronounced sagely, making for the kitchen.

When she carried in the tray, Vernon and Mary had got together on the smaller sofa, while Jimmy lay back, eyes closed, on the three-seater. Someone had switched on her portable radio and music played softly in the background.

The tea seemed to revive them, but Bella knew just how tired the men were. She looked worriedly at the clock. It was nearing midnight and Mary, small-built and fair-haired, shook Vernon's arm.

'Cinderella time coming up,' she joked. 'Hope you don't turn into a frog on the stroke of twelve, Vernon.'

He sprang to his feet. 'It's only Prince Charmings who do that,' he pointed out. 'Come on, love. I'll deliver you home safe and sound.'

'I've just remembered, Bella,' Mary said as they were leaving, 'the other day I was looking through one of the glossy magazines we've got on display, and guess who I saw? A photo of your boss and his lady love.'

Bella's heart sank. 'Reece, with Marguerite?'

Mary nodded. 'Looking lovey-dovey for the camera. At some fashion show or something. She'd designed the clothes, he'd provided the back-up.'

'Money, you mean?'

'Can't think what else the reporter meant.'

So Reece went around financing people's ventures, did he? Especially, no doubt, female ventures. See? she reproached herself severely. It wasn't just for me. But something inside her cried softly.

'Hey, brother,' Vernon said, 'we're off. How about you?'

There was no response from the sleeping figure.

'Sh-sh,' said Bella. 'Don't wake him suddenly.'

'He's not *sleep-walking*, silly.' Mary laughed, pulling Vernon behind her.

The music played on as Bella sat patiently, waiting for Jimmy to awaken. Growing anxious, she crossed to the sofa where he lay full-length and tapped his shoulder. It had no effect, so she stroked his hair, then tapped his cheek with her finger.

'Go ahead,' a voice grated from the doorway. 'Kiss Sleeping Beauty awake. That's what he's waiting for, isn't it? Along with all the other favours you've promised him tonight in my absence.'

Bella, startled out of her wits, jumped up, heart pounding, then sinking to rock-bottom. She and Jimmy weren't the only ones who were tired. The newcomer's eyes were shadowed with fatigue, his cheeks rough with stubble as if night driving had made it grow more quickly.

Tired or not, anger was in every line of him. 'What were you intending to do, sneak him into your bedroom, having assumed that I wouldn't be returning until tomorrow?'

Bella heard Jimmy stirring. Glancing over her shoulder, she saw him swing his long legs to the ground and sit, head in hands.

'Don't deny that you "want" him. I heard you say as much on the phone the other day.'

'No, no, you don't understand. That was——'

Behind her, Jimmy groaned. 'Oh, my, Bella love, I've got a wow of a hangover.' He groped the air and Bella caught his hand, pulling him up. 'Sorry, Bella.' His fluttering glance barely took in the presence of a stranger. 'Just see me to my van, will you?'

'I'll drive you, Jimmy,' Bella offered on the way.

'Thanks, Bella, but it's not really a hangover, I'm just dead tired.' At the wheel, his smile, more alert now from the impact of the fresh air, reassured her. 'I'll be OK.'

'I can't thank you enough, Jimmy, for all the work you've done for me.'

'Don't try, Bella. Let's call it a labour of love, shall we? See you.'

He drove away slowly into the night.

Bella dreaded the inevitable meeting with her enemy. He was prowling in the hall, confronting her forcefully as she entered. He looked as dangerous as the tiger Jacqueline had called him and she eyed the way to her rooms with longing. But a great barrier had to be surmounted before she would be allowed to reach that sanctuary. A barrier in the shape of a furious male, tie discarded, eyes castigating as they roamed over her dishevelled state.

She had not changed out of her working clothes, and her shirt, for coolness and greater freedom of movement, hung loose from the waistband of her dusty jeans. She knew there were smears on her cheeks and that her hair, uncombed for hours, looked as though a gale had played hairdresser and styled it crazily.

'So, because I'm home unexpectedly early,' he rasped with cutting sarcasm, 'you've been forced to spend the night alone? My heart bleeds for you. Well,' a step brought him threateningly near, 'that can be remedied with no difficulty at all.'

Fists on hips, he surveyed her. Then, before she could draw breath, she was in his arms. His hand thrust high beneath the loose blouse, roaming uninhibitedly, slipping round to her back and, with expert fingers, unhooking her bra.

He cut off her gasp with cruel lips, parting hers and savouring her sweet moistness, and all the while his palms stroked and moulded the fullness of her burgeoning shape, finding her nipples and forcing from her a frenzied response. She could not find it in her to pull away, to utter the 'no' with which to repel him.

Her arms made their own way around his neck, her fingers went walkabout in his travel-ruffled hair. There was about him the smell of other people's tobacco smoke, reminding her just how long he had been absent from her life.

Now he was finding the fastening of her jeans and, defenceless as she was in the overpowering strength of his embrace, she could not force herself to take any action to deflect him from his purpose.

When his hand moved with shivering intimacy down, over her hips, her stomach and, boldly, to her inner thighs, she pressed her burning cheek against the roughness of his chest hairs which had been revealed when her hands had found their trembling way to the fastenings of his shirt buttons.

'Reece,' she moaned, 'oh, please——'

'Take you?' Hard fingers gripped her chin and forced back her head. His eyes were frightening in their burning intensity and there seemed not to be an ounce of mercy in him. He carried her to the sofa and dropped her on to it, lying over her and letting her feel his unmistakable arousal.

'With the greatest pleasure,' he ground out, 'I'll give you what I deprived you of by my untimely arrival. And,' he added grimly, with his palms imprisoning her cheeks, holding her mesmerised gaze, 'having me in your bed will not break that contract you signed, which means you'll remain in my employ and also do me a service which you seem only too willing to provide, whatever the identity of the male who desires you, but which is not usually considered part of the duties of a live-in housekeeper. But since you're so eager, why should I bother to take you to bed?' He had unzipped her jeans and, moving to one side, began to jerk them from her. 'I'll have you here and now.'

A few more minutes, in fact only as long as it would take him to remove his own coverings, she would be his, irrevocably and totally. Yet his heart belonged to another woman, which meant that he would be using her only to purge himself of his anger with her for what he was certain she had intended to do in his absence.

She couldn't let it happen! Yet, when his mouth came down and suckled the hard pink peaks of her breasts, she could only gasp out his name and prepare herself for the point of no return.

There came a scream of a bell into the air. Someone was calling and that phone call had to be answered. Reece paused momentarily, but it seemed he intended to ignore it. Well, it was her phone, wasn't it, so it must be for her—her father maybe, needing her help?

With a strength she did not know she had, she levered herself from beneath him, hitting the floor with a bump that momentarily stunned her. Evading his angry hand, she ran to the phone, holding her blouse together with a shaking hand.

'Bella?' said the voice. 'Just thought I'd let you know I got home safe and sound.'

It was a chance in a million and she had to take it. What if it did confirm in Reece's mind that she had indeed intended to let her visitor stay the night?

'Oh, Jimmy dear, I'm so glad you rang. I wouldn't have slept a wink with worry in case you'd had an accident or something.' She heard Reece moving about but dared not turn and meet his eyes. 'I sound strange? Well, I feel OK.' He would never know how her world was falling in ruins about her. 'Just pleased you got home safely. Sleep well, Jimmy dear. Bye.'

Jimmy had sounded so pleased by her warm response to his call that Bella wondered if, in stopping something which had rapidly been slipping out of her control, she had started something else that might prove just as difficult to stop.

She forced her head up, facing Reece, but his eyes held such fury, such deep contempt that she wished she hadn't. Pale, tired beyond words, she looked at him.

'I'm glad you're back safe and sound, Mr Denman,' she said, in a tone that any housekeeper might use to her employer on his return from his travels.

His look was so cold she wrapped her arms around herself, and watched with despair in her heart as he swung to the door and left her.

'Jimmy, there's something missing,' Bella declared, looking round the 'village store' she and the Canfords had created and of which they were inordinately proud.

Jimmy shook his head. He had come next morning at Bella's request to take a last look around before the little shop was opened to the public. 'What, for instance? Wines and spirits? I remember your dad used to sell those.'

At the mention of her father's name, Bella glanced through the entrance arch and waved to him. Edgar returned it, having already promised to come over later and inspect her handiwork. 'That's Dad's department,' she explained. 'I couldn't set up in competition, could I?'

Jimmy glanced about him. 'I thought you'd offered Polly a job as your assistant?'

'I did. She's been away. She'll be in tomorrow.'

Jimmy nodded, looking strangely preoccupied.

'Bella?' he said at last. 'Last night when I rang you, you called me "dear" and seemed so pleased to hear from me. Does that mean, Bella, that you and I——?'

'Jimmy,' she broke in gently, 'last night, I——' It was terrible, she reproached herself, having to disappoint this very pleasant young man. How could she have used him the night before to protect herself from Reece's relentless and fiery lovemaking? 'Last night I'd had a drink or two. I——I don't quite remember exactly what I said. I was so relieved to hear you'd got home safely, I just—might—have given the wrong impression?'

'OK, Bella.' He had seemed to half expect her response. 'We'll stay friends, though, won't we?'

'Of course, Jimmy. Why not?'

Voices in the main store were raised in greeting, in deferential salutation to the striding newcomer who, Bella knew by instinct, was the man everyone called 'the boss'. She had not seen him that morning.

When, with trepidation, she had made her way to the kitchen to prepare breakfast, she had found to her relief that Reece had been there before her. His used dishes had been stacked on the dishwasher, the daily paper folded unevenly as if an irritable hand had scanned it and pushed it aside.

It seemed that the owner of those driving footsteps had no intention of stopping until they took him to his destination. And there could be no doubt at all that that was the 'village store' which, freshly painted and glorying in its 'new' old-fashioned fitments, waited patiently for the custom its creator was certain would come its way.

Then he was in front of her. Bella braced herself for the criticism she was sure was poised on the cynical lips of this man who was her sponsor and financial backer, especially in view of the presence of the man he was convinced was her lover, as indeed the rest of the town seemed to be convinced. No... correction, she thought ruefully, *one* of her lovers.

'What do you think of it, Mr Denman?' Jimmy asked, detaching himself from Bella.

'Congratulations on the result,' Reece said briskly.

Bella's eyes lit up. 'You like it, then? Jimmy and Vernon and I—we did it between us.'

His eyes flicked coolly to Bella's companion, then settled on her.

'I like it. The most important question is,' his head indicated the store beyond the screens, 'will the customers?'

*   *   *

Bella made a mental note as she tidied Reece's bed: see to all the household duties before you rush off to work every morning.

Smoothing the cover, her hand lingered on it, her eyes staring at the pillow and trying to imagine what Reece looked like when he was asleep. A rush of sheer, un-adulterated love swept over her and she had to close her eyes as his very personal aroma reached her nostrils. It was almost as though he was there.

He *was* there. He leaned against the wall near the door idly watching, suit jacket hanging loose, eyes hooded, tie dangling from his pocketed hands.

'Were my thoughts and those of my housekeeper similar?' He advanced slowly. 'What does Miss Harrison look like when she's asleep? Better still, wide awake and lying there, wearing all the clothes she was born in, arms outstretched and eager for her lover?'

His hands were freed from their prisons, the tie falling to the floor. Long fingers closed over her shoulders and impelled her towards him. 'Shall we satisfy each other's curiosity?' His gaze slipped to her lips and she knew what was coming, which meant she had to get away. Much more and he'd know her secret. Hadn't he guessed her thoughts?

'No, I——'

But his mind was on her capture, not her escape, and where his mind roamed his masculine strength went, too. And so did Bella, right into his arms, pulled hard against the angles of his body, unable to evade his seeking, testing mouth. Unable, too, to disguise her delight in the way his touch was drawing her deepest desires from their secret hiding-places, his hands beneath her blouse making free with the softly swelling shapes they knew so well by now...stroking and finger-trailing all over her throbbing flesh, slowly and very surely wearing away all of her resistance to his demands.

When he finally released her, she covered her burning cheeks and gazed up at him, still dazed by what had taken place, but, loving him though she did—he was only playing with her, wasn't he?—she knew what had to be said.

'I'm here as your housekeeper, Mr Denman, not your woman. If it happens again, I'll have to leave.' She cursed the faltering note, but it had escaped her control.

His eyes narrowed. 'I don't mistake an invitation when it's so blatantly offered me. You set it up. You take the consequences.'

'Set it up? Invitation? What are you talking about?' she asked wildly. 'I was in here doing my job, which was making your bed.'

'Which you deliberately left until I returned home.'

'You really think that of me? It's the end now, Mr Denman,' she countered. 'If you don't trust me . . .' She had reached the door. He hadn't moved, just watched darkly, hands on hips. 'In my own defence,' she got out shakily, 'and for the sake of any future reference I might ask you to provide on my character, I'll tell you why I was here. I didn't hear your car. I ran straight up here as soon as I got home because I hadn't had time this morning to tidy your room. From tomorrow morning onwards, I've made a promise to myself to see to everything domestic before I leave.'

He still seemed unconvinced, so she abandoned defence and went on to the attack.

'If you'll excuse me, *sir*,' she said, defying the anger that sprang into this eyes, 'I'll get your evening meal, then tidy my own rooms. You see, I've invited my friends for the evening. Male, if I'm allowed?' She paused a moment as if for permission. All she received was a narrowed stare. 'And female—that is, if you don't object to my having friends?'

'You can cut out the sarcasm,' was his curt rejoinder.

She half opened the door then turned back to him. 'Reece?'

He looked at her coldly.

'I've thought of a name for my little shop. Bella's Food Basket.'

A pause, then, 'So?'

She hid her disappointment at his response by lifting her head. Why had she thought he might warmly approve?

'I know you're beginning to doubt the wisdom of the whole venture. I know by your remark this morning about whether the customers will like it. I also know that you're secretly wondering if you've been too hasty in helping me like this and whether you've wasted your money.'

His eyebrows leapt high. 'You know all this? You've found a secret tunnel into the depths of my mind?'

She let his sarcasm pass over her. 'I'm going to give this project everything I've got. I'm going *make* my little shop-within-a-shop succeed.'

CHAPTER TEN

IT WAS harder keeping her promise than Bella had thought. The first few days were the worst. Polly busied herself taking stock from the displays, pretending to carry it away, then returning it to the shelves.

'I've got to look busy,' she told an increasingly dismayed Bella, 'for my job's sake as well as yours. You just stand there and look pretty. No, no, don't frown,' she cautioned, 'smile for all you're worth. Look, here's a customer.' Polly peered over the centre stands. 'She's looking. Oh, she's gone away.' She shook her head and continued with her 'work'.

'Tomorrow they'll come,' Bella said bravely. 'They just haven't noticed we're here.'

'If only it were Christmas,' Polly sighed. 'We could put up decorations and rows of coloured lights. Anything, I'd say, to attract attention.'

Each evening that week Bella went home dreading that Reece might ask for sales figures, question her about how things were going. It seemed he had forgotten all about Bella's Food Basket. He was distant and businesslike, breakfasting before she was up and frequently dining in town. Miserably, Bella wondered just who he was dating, then told herself not to be stupid, she knew very well. He just couldn't resist the beautiful Marguerite's charms.

Polly was at lunch when Bella, desperately trying to rearrange some displays in order to show them to their best advantage, heard the sound of a customer. Eagerly she turned, her heart sinking fathoms down at the sight of Malcolm Haddern.

He was smiling, having placed a couple of soft drink cans under Bella's nose. He put some coins on the imitation wooden counter, then leaned comfortably against it.

'How's business?' He seemed politeness itself and Bella felt a *frisson* of fear pass over her. 'I've heard on the grapevine that Food Basket isn't, as yet, on the shoppers' map.'

You can say that again, she thought. 'Well, I—we're still waiting to be noticed. Why?'

'Chin up, Bella. I'm here to help you,' he said with a pleasant smile which Bella instinctively mistrusted. 'My line's public relations. I meet a lot of people, I—er,' he pushed around the change Bella had given him, 'I could put a lot of custom your way.'

It was the way he said it that made Bella bristle. 'I don't need help, thanks. These things take time.' But how long can you afford to wait? a persistent voice asked. It won't be long before Reece is breathing down your neck...

'You're hesitating, Bella?'

She shook her head fiercely. Had he read her worry in her eyes? 'I'm certainly not.'

'Ah, come on. We could talk it over, Bella. I'm free tonight. How about you? We could drive to a restaurant, eat a bit, drink a bit. Talk. Then—er—who knows? Yes?'

'No! Thank you.'

'Come on,' he coaxed again. 'It'd be worth your while, Bella. Just imagine,' his arm swept round, taking in the whole empty area, 'this place full of people fighting each other to get to the goodies. Faces smiling because they're in a warm, cosy atmosphere, instead of out there in a great big impersonal store. No frantic hassle at the check-outs, just little Miss Harrison, and her sweet little assistant there to take their money. Yes, I can see you like the idea. An evening spent with me.'

She cursed the longing her eyes had betrayed at his sweet talk and persuasive tactics. 'Of course I like the idea of Food Basket being a success. But as for using a date with you to help——'

He broke in before she could refuse him with greater vigour. 'It'd be worth it, Bella,' he urged with a sugar-sweet smile, 'in terms of financial returns and just plain happiness at seeing Bella's Food Basket filled to over-flowing. And, sweetie,' his voice lowered, 'I wouldn't do anything you didn't want. I understand a lady's needs...'

She took a breath. At Malcolm's persuasive words, the vision that had flashed before her mind had been captivating and wonderful.

'Thank you for your kind offer,' she answered briskly, 'but I'm not that sort——'

'No?' The true Malcolm Haddern surfaced frighteningly. His mouth worked. 'So whose little bed-mate are you, then?' He counted on his fingers. 'Canfords, Jimmy and Vernon. Strangor-Denman, Reece.'

'No!' It came too quickly, too anxiously.

'No?' he sneered. 'You're his housekeeper, aren't you? He bought out your business, set you up here, *and* he's taking your losses on the chin without a murmur. Think he doesn't know? And you try to tell me you and he sleep in separate rooms? Yeah?' His fingers tapped thoughtfully on the counter. 'I'll say it once more. I can bring Bella Harrison custom, profits and success. Say just one little "yes, Malc", and it's all hers. How about it, then?'

'Go jump off Everest, Mr Haddern,' Bella answered, speaking each word clearly. 'And I hope nobody, but nobody, hears your cries for help. The answer is no. And that's final.'

He drew a growling breath, seized his goods with a threatening gesture and stamped away.

Since Reece had not instructed her to the contrary, Bella assumed once again that she would not have to cook an evening meal. She didn't feel hungry so she decided to miss out on one herself.

Disconsolately she wandered round the grounds, through the heavily scented rose gardens, across the lawns, then back, finding her way to the patio and seating herself beneath the brightly coloured parasol. It was here, she remembered, that Reece had kissed her on the night of Jacqueline's and Dick's engagement party. He'd sat there, next to her, and somehow life had seemed so good . . .

She folded her arms on the table and rested her aching head, letting the tears fall, of disappointment and hopelessness, of puzzlement at human nature—why should everyone walk by her little shop as though it didn't even exist?

On arriving home, she had phoned her father. 'It isn't good, lass,' he'd commiserated. 'I've been watching and you could count on the fingers of one hand the people who've patronised you each day. Don't be surprised if——'

'Reece puts up the "closing down" notice? Oh, Dad, what am I to do?'

'Just hold the fort, Bella, and keep on trying until the axe falls.'

Which, Bella had thought, putting down the phone and rubbing her neck, had been a somewhat unfortunate phrase.

Then there was Malcolm Haddern. He'd seemed so annoyed at her rejection of him she couldn't help wondering if, having done his worst last time, there was anything he might try to do now in revenge for her latest angry brush-off. But he couldn't make her situation any worse, could he? She was on her way out of Columbine's store anyway.

'Bella?'

She tensed with fright, which lasted only seconds, to be succeeded by a guilty conscience that she hadn't cooked a single bit of food for her employer. 'I thought you were eating out again. You should have told me.'

Was this the moment when the axe, as her father had called it, was going to fall? To her surprise, he did not seem to be on the warpath. Which could just mean that, work-wise, she might live to see another day!

He sat beside her and leaned forward to remove a tear or two on to his forefinger, examining his catch and smiling sardonically. 'What are these for? Unrequited love?'

He was far too near the truth! 'H-how do you mean?'

'Jimmy Canford? On my way home, I saw him out with Polly.'

She felt relief that he was on the wrong track. 'You did?' Jimmy and Polly? It had never occurred to her. Yet Jimmy had asked about her, hadn't he?

'No, I'm——' She moistened her lips. 'I didn't re-alise.' The idea pleased her. They'd go well together. And it meant that he hadn't taken her gentle rejection of him too much to heart.

She leaned back, sighing, patting her cheeks dry with a tissue she had found in her jeans pocket. She scraped back the chair. 'I'll cook you something. It may take half an hour, but while you wait you could have a drink and some crisps, couldn't you?'

'I could. And so could you. Before our meal at the Silver Moon.' He rose, glancing at his watch. 'Ten minutes to change. And,' with his hand he covered her lips which were parting in protest, 'no objections.'

Like magic, her spirits rose and she sped upstairs. The Silver Moon was an upmarket country inn with a well-known cuisine. She sought out the dress she had worn for Jacqueline's party. She hadn't had time to add to her wardrobe since moving into Windham House.

Now Reece sat opposite her at a secluded candle-lit table set apart from other diners, on a shallow platform beside a great gilt-framed mirror.

'Why?' Bella asked, wishing the lowered lighting did not shed so many shadows, one of which at that moment had half hidden her companion's face.

'Why this, you mean? Why are we dining together? Why not?'

Her slender shoulder lifted, but that had been the wrong thing to do, because it attracted Reece's interested eyes. 'I wanted to talk to you. This seemed the best place to do it.'

It came to her then, the reason why they were there.

They had given their order and, as they waited, Bella toyed with the bread roll she had accepted from the waitress. As she tore at it, she steeled herself for Reece's statement: I'm closing Bella's Food Basket.

'It's been a failure, hasn't it?' To salve her battered pride she had said it first.

He pretended to look baffled and a little hurt. 'But the evening's just begun. Give it time, Bella.'

'You know what I mean,' she persisted. 'You've seen the sales figures, you must have. Hardly anything to show for the whole week. I don't blame you,' she rushed on, 'for abandoning the whole venture. I'm glad I didn't employ expensive workers. The Canford brothers' fees are very reasonable, so you won't have lost too much.'

He retreated into shadow. 'You're giving up? After five days? I thought Isabella Harrison was made of sterner stuff.'

Her heart began to jump. 'You mean, you're not——'

'I'm not. Whenever did a new venture show a profit in five days?'

Their meal arrived. 'Let's eat,' Reece suggested.

She looked at her filled plate, shaking her head. 'I'm just not——' But she was, ravenously. The world was suddenly a brighter place. Reece still had faith in her, he was willing to give her more time to prove her worth and that of Bella's Food Basket.

He waited until the end of the meal to put his idea to her. 'You need to make an impact. When Columbine's opened its refurbished doors, we had a grand opening. So, to put Bella's Food Basket on the map, we'll have a "mini grand opening". What do you say to an old-style garden fête, to go with an old-style shop?'

Bella stared at him, hardly daring to believe her ears. 'I'd say "yes, please". You'd do that for——?' 'Me', she had almost said, but reminded herself that it would be in his interests to make certain that his investment in her was a financial success. 'But that would cost you a fortune,' she added worriedly.

'Hardly.' He took her hand. 'But it would pay dividends—in other ways.'

'Moneywise, of course.' She had been right in her guess regarding his motives, after all.

'But of course. What else did you think I meant?'

Had she detected a note of amusement? She glanced up but his expression was as informative as a blank page.

As he replaced her hand on her side of the table, her side vision was caught by the reflection in the mirror beside them of a figure flitting past. Her head turned quickly, but the person had gone.

Of course it hadn't been Malcolm Haddern! The man was haunting her. Anyway, even if it had been, knowing as she did now that Reece was willing to be patient over the results of their joint venture, there was nothing Malcolm Haddern could do to harm her.

'Come over to the enemy.' Reece caught her wrist as, on arriving home, she made to leave him for her part of the house.

She had no option but to go with him to his living-room, her heart hammering. 'You mean you're aware of your role in my life?' she queried with an impudent smile.

'Oh, yes. Haven't you taken every opportunity in the past, not forgetting the present, to let me know that, in your eyes, the town's divided into two—your side, and "the other side"?'

'Yet here I am, on that "other side".' She raised a bright-eyed face to his.

'As an employee—yes? On sufferance—yes, again?'

'Yes and yes. Because otherwise I wouldn't have a home.'

'Blunt and to the point. That's Bella Harrison.' He removed his jacket and pulled her down on to a sofa, leaning against his corner, arms folded, and watching as she settled into hers. 'A two-cushion distance between us. Which,' he pretended to estimate, 'is about right for a business discussion.'

Stop it, Bella told her treacherous heart, stop diving to ground-level. What else did you think this man had in mind? 'The meal—it was great,' was all she could think of to break the silence. 'Thanks a lot for it.'

'Strictly business, Miss Harrison. It will appear on my expenses sheet.' His fingers were playing a soundless piano piece on the upholstered arm of the sofa, while his eyes seemed to have difficulty drawing themselves away from the expanse of white skin which the wide neckline of her dress revealed.

OK, sink, she told her wavering spirits; so he's smiling, but you can be sure he's speaking the truth.

'About this garden fête you mentioned,' she said, determined to play the game his way and keep the conversation on an impersonal level. 'When and where?'

'Right.' When Reece Denman turns businessman, Bella thought, glad he had taken up her cue, but foolishly disappointed all the same, all emotion and familiarity vanish. 'Here, I think. In the grounds of Windham House.' He sat back, legs crossed, fingers still drumming, his tie thrown aside and his white shirt straining against the breadth of his shoulders.

His eyes half closed as he visualised the proceedings. 'We'll hire caterers and a marquee. We'll invite the Press, public relations people——'

'Not—not Malcolm Haddern.'

'Oh?' He was coolly surprised. 'Why not? He's an old friend. Also, he's got contacts on his list who could do us—you—a lot of good.'

Which had to mean that Malcolm had been speaking the truth when he'd told her, 'I could put a lot of custom your way.' So how could she explain to Reece that his 'old friend' had tried to proposition her and also that she couldn't stand the sight of him?

She looked at her twisting foot. 'You know best.'

'Thanks a lot,' he returned drily.

Some time later, Bella stifled a yawn, but Reece had noticed. He rose, standing in front of her, hands slipped into his belt.

'I'm tiring my housekeeper. Time for bed. Pity she insists on spending all her nights alone.' Bella stood, too, finding herself disquietingly near to the face she had grown to love. 'Living with your "enemy", Bella—how does it grab you?'

Terrific, great, unimaginably wonderful... The words didn't make it to her lips, but she couldn't be sure what message her eyes were conveying.

His arms sprang to life, his eyes blazing a message of desire that had her swaying. He wrapped her round in an iron-hard embrace and impelled her head back with the strength of his kiss. He was sweeping her with him, taking her on a road which had no side turnings, and from which she could escape only by turning back.

'Bella, Bella,' he said thickly, 'you're so fresh, so fine, I can't believe you're what they say you are.'

It was like an earthquake shaking her world. It meant that, deep inside him, he still believed her to be promiscuous and over-free with her favours. She wanted to cry out to him that she had never let a man...never wanted a man enough until now, until he...

The telephone shrilled, cooling the feverish movements, the hand caressing her breasts withdrawing, all intimate contact broken.

'Yes?' Reece barked into the receiver. 'Who? Malc? Get lost, pal, will you? What?' His head swivelled round. 'Yes, she's here. With me. Why?'

Malcolm's voice came small but sharp into the room. 'I saw you in the Silver Moon. A cosy twosome, lovey-dovey. What was she promising you, old friend? What she half promised me this afternoon?'

'It's not true!' Bella cried. 'He propositioned me, saying he'd put custom my way if I dated him, then afterwards...' Her voice trailed away. At the ice in Reece's eyes, she added, 'I said no. Believe me, I did.'

'I heard that,' said Malcolm's raised voice. 'There are ways of saying no, lady—a real brush-off, or the hesitant "maybe if you keep pressing me and I get something out of it" kind. Yours was the latter, no mistaking it. Well, whadderyouknow?' he exclaimed, as if the thought had just hit him. 'That girl must be something! Tell me,

Reece, old pal, is she easy on the bank account? Girls from that end of the town usually are, if you get my meaning. Put me on to her, pal. Give me a chance.'

Reece held out the telephone as if its touch had tainted his hand.

Bella seized it. 'Get off my back, Mr Haddern,' she spat, 'or I'll get you for slander, do you hear?'

Malcolm's raucous laughter was cut off only when she dropped the receiver on to its rack. She swung to face Reece, head high.

'I suppose that's convinced you, Mr Denman, that I'm as *bad* as they're all saying I am. I know you won't believe me if I say that never once did I contemplate going anywhere with your *old friend* Malcolm Haddern. I must admit that his offer to put custom my way was attractive, but the price I'd have had to pay was not one I'd touch with protective gloves a mile thick.'

Inscrutable eyes raked her, a hard jaw thrust forward. 'So what would be your price, Miss Harrison, for a night in your bed? Name it, money no object, and I'll make financial arrangements with your bank tomorrow.'

With a cry, she swung her hand, aiming at his cheek. His lightning reaction stopped it before it made contact, his fingers unbearably tight around her wrist.

He released her at last and she stepped away, rubbing her bruised skin. By the set of his jaw and the repudiation in his eyes, she knew that, as far as their mutual harmony was concerned, things would never be the same again.

From that evening on, Reece was cold and distant. Bella soothed her savaged pride by behaving impeccably as housekeeper and employee, keeping all her responses to his requests and requirements as impassive and deadpan as possible.

She had not realised before how a man and a woman could live together in a house, yet remain as strangers, passing sometimes without even a nod of recognition. She did not know how long Reece could keep it up, but she knew that the whole impossible situation was tearing her to pieces.

It had begun to affect not only her appetite but her feeling of well-being, too. The strain being as bad as it was, on her side at least, she was aware that something soon would have to give.

When Reece had need to discuss with her the plans for the fast-approaching garden fête, he asked her to attend him at his office in the town. Often others were present, caterers and florists, advertising executives called in for the purpose of publicising the event. They all asked for her suggestions and ideas, promising to incorporate them with theirs.

There were numerous evenings when Reece had company at home, friends or business acquaintances to dinner, when she would have to act the perfect house-keeper and keep a smile on her face. She was now excluded from every aspect of his private life, except as his employee.

He did not, of course, go short of female company, chiefly in the form of Marguerite Hunter-Parkes. Bella often had to open the door to the lady guest, tall and gracious, looking down her shapely nose at the house-keeper who came from the side of the town which she, Marguerite, rarely set foot in.

So bitter did Bella become about Reece's changed attitude towards her, especially as it was so completely unjust and unjustified, she invited into her part of the house her own set of friends, boldly risking his dis-pleasure by allowing them sometimes to stay until midnight.

Often when she came to show them out, late though it was, Marguerite's car would still be in the driveway. On those nights, she would go miserably to bed, tossing and turning and wondering whether she would have to provide breakfast for two in the morning.

Now and then she invited Jimmy on his own. Despite his growing friendship with Polly, he still appeared to nourish a secret hope that Bella might one day change her mind about him.

The weather had turned wet and cool for the time of year and, as she and Jimmy one evening watched the late film, Bella heard the rain lashing down and the wind howling round the old house.

The film over, Jimmy glanced at his watch and exclaimed, 'Gone one! It's tomorrow morning, Bella.'

'Today, you mean.' She stretched, yawning, having enjoyed the romance woven into the story, her thoughts still wrapped around with it.

In the hall, as Jimmy bent down for a routine goodnight kiss on her cheek, Bella heard a sound nearby and turned her head, Jimmy's mouth landing unexpectedly on hers.

Closing the door against the force of the gale, Bella leaned against it tiredly, hearing another sound. She turned swiftly and saw Reece staring at her, eyes piercing through the semi-darkness. Anger erupted within her, uncontrollable and devastating in its strength, all the more so because of the way she had all these past unbearable days kept it so firmly battened down.

'What are you doing?' she asked shrilly. 'Keeping tabs on my visitors and the time they leave? Are you so eager to implement that clause you put into my contract that you're actually *spying* on me? Don't worry, I'll save you the bother. I'll pack in the morning and leave.' She swung towards her section of the house. 'Come along to my bedroom if you want to, Mr Strangor-Denman, and look at how my bed's all rumpled and jumbled up with our— with my and Jimmy's *activities*.'

He hadn't moved, nor displayed a single glimpse of emotion. She could not stand his implacability another second. Before she knew what her feet were up to, they had taken her back along the hall. They must have been in league with her arms and her hands, because she discovered that they were battering his chest like a punch-drunk boxer knowing victory was slipping out of his grasp.

He still did not move, letting her fists have their way, taking their impact as if they were moths hitting an uncurtained window-pane in a futile attempt to break through it.

'I hate you,' she gasped, 'I hate you so much I'd like to—to——'

A hand closed over her mouth, while another deftly caught her two wrists, imprisoning them in a punishing grasp. She found he was shaking her, and it was only when her head began to nod painfully with the movement that she came to her senses and collapsed against him, cheek against his chest, arms limply around his waist.

The tears came then, tears she had refused to allow to surface for all the time of their silent battle, and she sobbed and swallowed and reached into her trouser pockets for a handkerchief.

It was only when at last she drew away that she realised his arms had remained at his sides all through her storm of weeping. She could not bring herself to raise her eyes to see his unmoved, unresponsive stare, and turned away with a mumbled apology, finding herself moments later alone in her living-room and lying, still sobbing, on a sofa.

Polly stayed with Bella the evening before the day of the fête.

'I heard,' Polly said, 'that there's going to be a replica of Bella's Food Basket. Is that right?'

Bella said it was. 'And a fashion show. Marguerite Hunter-Parkes—know her?'

'You mean Reece Denman's girlfriend?'

Bella nodded, hiding her pain at the admission. 'She's calling her show Nostalgia Unlimited. Mixing modern fashion with a hint of decades gone by. Hoping to start a trend, I was told. She's bringing a "famous name" to open the fête, Reece told me. A lady actress friend of hers.'

Drying the dishes that evening, Polly glanced anxiously through the kitchen windows.

'The forecast wasn't that good for tomorrow. Windy, wet, but with some sun. Hope that marquee out there is good and strong. Wouldn't all our guests look great if the rain came through the canvas, or whatever, and soaked them?'

Bella laughed with her, but it did not relieve the tension she had felt building up in her over the days since her one-sided but none the less bitter quarrel with Reece.

In the intervening time, he had been absent more than present in the house, but even when he was there his cold manner towards her made her wish sometimes that he had gone as usual—where else would he spend so much time and so many nights?—to his lady-friend's in London.

The morning dawned bright, clear and very windy.

'Just right for jackets over summer dresses,' Polly had declared, watching the caterers carrying in boxes of crockery and hygienically packaged food, while the florists delivered vanloads of flowers and supplies.

The marquee stretched wide and high, generously straddling the lawns, waiting for the eager crowds to fill it.

'How do I look?' Polly asked her own reflection in Bella's full-length mirror. Her dress was multi-striped and slenderly cut to fit her slim figure.

'Just great,' Bella replied, adding wickedly, 'Jimmy'll love it.'

'Hey,' Polly swung round, turning pink, 'there's nothing in it, I swear. I like him, he likes me, that's all. I——' hesitantly she added '—I don't want to take him away from you.'

Bella smiled reassuringly. 'We've always been just friends, honestly.'

'Thanks a lot, Bella,' Polly returned happily, then looked admiringly at Bella's linen-look shirtwaister dress with its touches of navy at collar and waist.

'Oh, Polly,' Bella clasped her hands, 'I hope this garden fête works, I hope it puts Bella's Food Basket on the shopping map.'

'You bet it will. Come on, boss,' Polly smoothed her hair and squared up as if for a fight, 'let's make our entrance and wow 'em out there.'

The crowds grew by the minute, the noise-level rose, and the wind strength with it. The fashion models on the catwalk swayed and danced to the recorded music, the wind's impact blowing their hems high to the shrieks of the girls and the laughter of the onlookers.

'Bella's Food Basket' was a roaring success, customers jostling each other to patronise the 'shop', some of them, Bella noticed with joy, being her customer friends from the old days.

Her father had gladly returned to his old job of serving behind the 'counter', Maddy Langridge happily helping him. Jimmy had come, turning odd-job man whenever repairs were needed. Vernon was there, holding Mary Walker's hand.

Reece, who had been away for a few days, had returned without warning, giving Bella a perfunctory nod and stopping over only for a shower and a change of clothes.

Bella was offering change to a customer who had purchased a pile of Food Basket's offerings when her heart did a swallow dive. 'Oh, no!' she exclaimed aloud. 'There's Malcolm Haddern. Who invited *him*?'

'I did,' answered a quiet masculine voice at her side and she nearly jumped out of her skin to find Reece beside her, hands in pockets, looking so handsome and tall, and yet so aloof and untouchable she could hardly bear it.

'I——' How should she answer? 'As long as he paid his entrance fee,' she commented as offhandedly as she could. 'Besides, he's your old friend, isn't he?'

Bella hadn't intended to sound sarcastic, but the intonation was there.

'You're so right,' Reece responded, in his turn sharply cynical, and moved away, pushing through the crush to reach Marguerite's side.

Towards the end of the afternoon, Bella thankfully snatched a rest on the patio. People were drifting away, now, the children excitedly holding the gifts their parents had bought them.

Her father approached, carefully carrying two mugs of tea from the snacks counter. He passed one to Bella, and she drank gratefully.

'All this, lass,' he waved towards the thinning crowds, 'should have put your little "shop" on the map. Everyone's going home now, but the Press was there—did you know?' He smiled at her fondly. 'Reece treating you all right, love?'

'Reece? Yes . . . yes, of course. Why do you ask?'

'Just that sometimes at work you look a bit pale and tired.' Bella was well aware of the reason for that, but not for the world would she let him into her secret. Edgar stirred his tea and Bella guessed that there was something on his mind. 'Bella, dear, Maddy and me. Have you noticed?' Bella, startled, shook her head. 'We—we like each other a lot. We've talked it over and we've decided to get married. We wanted you to be the first to know.'

'Oh, Dad,' Bella hugged him tightly, 'I'm so glad, so happy for you both. When's it to be?'

'Dear me, lass, you're in a hurry! At our age, there's no rush.' He patted her hand, laughing, and left.

'Bella.' She looked up quickly. It was a voice that never failed to set her pulses racing. Reece stood beside the chair her father had vacated.

He lifted a foot to rest on the seat and leant forward on an elbow. The wind played with the parasol above, blew scraps of paper and discarded containers, tossed Bella's hair in front of her eyes. His glance slanted down at her. 'Name your charity.'

She looked at him questioningly. 'You mean, the money raised here won't——'

'Go into my bank account. No. Which one?'

She was overwhelmed. 'Which charity? I don't really know. There are so many that need help.'

'OK, make a list some time and we'll divide the proceeds equally between them.'

Her face glowed up at him. 'It's very good of you to be so public-spirited. All this, too, to help my little shop. Not that it's mine of course,' she amended quickly. He seemed about to speak but must have sensed they were not alone. He removed his foot from the chair and looked round.

Jimmy hovered and Reece glanced from him to Bella. He nodded at the newcomer and strode away. Bella's eyes clung to his lithe, retreating figure, admiring his long-limbed walk, following his every footstep. He battled and won against the strong wind which reached almost gale force at times, flapping at his jacket and messing up his hair.

When Bella eventually tore her eyes away, Jimmy was seated, drawing a carton of fruit juice from his pocket and proceeding to drink from it through a straw.

'It's him, isn't it?' The words came between gulps, catching Bella off guard.

'I—you—what do you mean, Jimmy?'

'Him, Reece Denman, who we all used to look on when we were kids together as "the enemy".'

'If you're implying I'm his ally now, that I've gone over to his side, it's not——'

Jimmy's hand patted hers. 'I mean, Bella, that he's the man you want. I understand. I accept it. No one knows who their hearts will settle on where liking and loving are concerned.'

Bella moved her empty mug around. 'I might—more than like him, Jimmy, but he's got eyes only for his lady-friend. I'm not in his league. Or his social circle.'

'I'm never going to be second best in a woman's life, Bella. You know that, don't you?'

She nodded. 'You're a fine man, Jimmy, and I like you very much. I only wish it could be more.'

Almost on cue, a rogue gust of wind filled the parasol above them and lifted it clean out of its socket. Jimmy chased it, bringing it back and inspecting it for damamge. He righted the table which had fallen over, and slid the errant parasol back into its socket, while Bella retrieved the empty mugs which had tumbled down, miraculously without breaking.

Jimmy smoothed his hair and stared across the lawns towards the stalls, easily visible now that the visitors had almost all gone.

He seemed to come to a decision. Standing, he turned to Bella, putting his arms round her shoulders, kissing her on the mouth. 'Thanks, Bella,' he said with a note of sadness, 'for everything.' He was saying goodbye.

Bella returned his kiss gently. 'Still friends, Jimmy, yes?'

He nodded, his eyes again straining across the lawns, no doubt, Bella thought, to see if Polly was still there.

'I don't think much of that marquee.' There was concern in his voice.

'Why, Jimmy?' Bella frowned. 'Can't say I've noticed anything different about it.'

'It's years out of date, flimsy construction, canvas not properly treated against rain. I heard Reece Denman say that Malcolm Haddern had offered to get a marquee for the great event. Knew of a good hiring firm, he said, through his PR contacts, and would negotiate a fair price. When Reece saw it for the first time this morning, he was furious, but couldn't do anything about it. If he'd been around when it was erected, he said, he'd have sent it back.'

Bella nodded. 'Reece only came back this morning. The caterers and florists started filling it yesterday.' Bella shrugged. 'Nobody seems to have noticed, so let's hope it stands up to this wind.'

'Hey, there, Polly,' Jimmy shouted, 'wait for me. See you, Bella,' he said and made a dash. Polly, looking round, took his hand and walked with him.

Bella stood for a few moments, closing her eyes, letting the past twenty minutes wash over her. First, her father's news, then Reece's donating the proceeds to charity. And now Jimmy. It wasn't easy, she thought, seeing someone walk out of your life, someone as familiar and kind as Jimmy Canford. It was as though a few pages had turned, a chapter ended. She shook off the momentary sadness and made for the marquee.

Dark clouds, driven by the strength of the gale, threatened rain and she looked around hoping everyone was as aware as she was of the imminent downpour.

The marquee was almost deserted. The great empty space was swirling with the gale-force wind as it rushed in in eddies, entering through 'doorways' and exiting through gaps and slits. The guy ropes that tethered the construction to earth shook and rattled outside.

Bella attempted to bring some order to the used crockery spread over the trestle-tables, wishing the wind would die down. A drumming noise above her head told her that the clouds had kept their promise and were depositing their moisture content well and truly on the remnants of the garden fête below.

Thank goodness, Bella was thinking, as she dived beneath the trestle-table to gather together the shattered pieces of a broken plate, the rain had held off until now.

As she emerged from under the table, a great and terrifying gust of wind moaned and shrieked through the billowing marquee, uplifting the soaking fabric and crashing the unstable construction all around her. She remembered Jimmy's critical comments about Malcolm's choice of marquee and realised how right he had been.

The table tipped crazily on to its side, its clattering contents shooting in all directions. Having had no time to straighten, Bella found herself sprawling face down beneath the heavy weight of the saturated canvas. She felt its leaden wetness descend all over her, trapping her completely.

She cried out for help, gritting her teeth and making a vain effort to stiffen her neck and hold her head up against the heavy weight that bore down on her prostrate figure. She found it increasingly difficult to breathe.

Panic which she tried her best to suppress rose within her, but it finally manifested itself in a series of screams which, she told her persistently rational self, at least made her lungs keep working and might even, with luck, tell anyone who was interested where she was.

When at last she became aware of voices, of her name being shouted, of running footsteps and a general movement of the unwelcome drapery that had wrapped itself around her, she realised that not for much longer could she keep at bay the unbelievable idea that, if help didn't come very soon, these might be the very last breaths she would be able to draw.

Which would be a pity, a terrible pity... the thoughts raced through her head before consciousness receded... because then she would never be able to convince Reece of the truth about herself. Worst of all, she would never be able to tell him that she loved him.

CHAPTER ELEVEN

SOMEONE was hefting a heavy weight from over Bella, freeing her nostrils to draw in air, rolling her on to her back. Someone was lifting her head, peering into her face.

'Bella. Can you hear me?' The voice was fraught with anxiety, anguished almost, a voice that was familiar and dear, and warm and vibrating with deep feeling. So whose voice was it? Not Reece's, because he would never speak to her like that, not to Bella Harrison, a girl from the other, lesser side of the town.

Her eyes flickered open and they saw that it was indeed the man she had thought it couldn't possibly be. But of course he was anxious. Hadn't this fête, this opening ceremony been his idea? Yes, her memory was coming back, supplying her with information about the immediate past.

She had come into the marquee, she'd been tidying up, then the whole world had collapsed about her. The man in whose arms she now seemed to be lying was her anchor, her sanctuary, her shelter from life's storms, so she clung to him fiercely. It was her only means of telling him that she needed him, how she loved him and that she never wanted him to let her go.

'Where's her father?' someone asked as those arms whisked her through the air.

'Gone home,' was the answer.

'Call a doctor.' There was Reece's voice again, giving orders and expecting them to be obeyed.

'Will do,' said a voice like Vernon's, accompanied by hurrying feet.

'Anyone else under this flaming contraption?' Jimmy's voice, fraught and angry.

'They all got out,' somebody told him.

Strong arms carried her indoors, their owner effortlessly sprinting up a flight of stairs and lowering her on to a bed. Her glance flickered round the room, taking in the fact that it was her own bedroom. Then they focused on Reece's face, pale, worried, close to hers as he stroked back her hair.

He's worried about *me*? The question, full of hope, drifted around her mind. Of course he is, came the down-to-earth answer. As his employee, you're his responsibility.

He felt her pulse, but she was sufficiently awake now to snatch her hand away. If he felt its speed, he would get alarmed, not knowing that it was racing only because he was touching her.

At her action, his expression closed down, his lips tautened and he went out. So she'd angered him. Well, better that than embarrassing him by revealing even in that small way her feelings for him. If only she could throw caution to the winds and confess by word and action her love for this man—her enemy—whom she found, always had, so irresistible.

The doctor came, Reece standing discreetly back while he carried out his examination. Cuts, bruises and some evidence of shock, he diagnosed, advising rest. He went away, Reece going with him, then returning to say that if she wanted him he would be outside with the others.

If she *wanted* him, he'd said. Well, she did, she wanted Reece back, wanted him in her arms... *wanted* him with a longing that hurt far more than the injuries she had sustained out there in the collapsed marquee.

As the evening passed, Reece came in once or twice, telling her that the almost continuous phone calls had mostly been enquiries about her state of health. He offered food and drink, but Bella refused everything.

Darkness came and she lay there remembering the afternoon. The opening ceremony, when Reece had presented the famous actress who, in turn, had introduced 'Bella of Bella's Food Basket'. Cameras had flashed, people had applauded, Reece had unbelievably taken her hand and allowed himself to be photographed with her.

Taking a shower, she dried herself carefully. The bruises, she noted, were emerging somewhat colourfully from beneath her skin. Sleep came after that and with it much needed rest, but it seemed she had not slept for long before she was awakened by voices raised in anger.

'I trusted you, Malcolm,' Reece was saying, plainly reining in his temper with difficulty, 'to hire the best, not the worst available. Nor to attend a sale of second-hand goods to find an out-of-date, below-standard product without today's built-in safeguards against storm damage.'

'So you aren't pleased that I saved you money? That I got the best at the price I thought you'd want to spend for the sake of that *tarnished* little——'

'*Saved* me money?' Reece broke in furiously. 'Don't you realise that if that girl up there wanted to she could sue me for negligence and heaven knows what else?'

Oh, no, Bella's breaking heart cried out, is that why he's been so worried, so attentive? Hoping to placate me so that I wouldn't think of taking him to law?

'Yeah, "that girl up there",' Malcolm sneered. 'Glad you're relegating her to her rightful place. You took her in as your housekeeper, OK, so you're employing her, and no doubt *enjoying* her. But never in a million years could a girl from that side of the town be your equal. Besides,' in a sulky tone, 'no woman treats me with contempt, nor gives me the sneering brush-offs that she's handed out to me, and gets away with it unscathed.'

So that was how Malcolm Haddern had taken his revenge! Shaking with anger, Bella scrambled from the bed and ran to the top of the curving staircase, pausing to regain her breath. It had exhausted her more than she had thought.

'For Pete's sake, Reece, old pal,' Malcolm cajoled, 'stop taking her into your bed, or she'll get ideas. Besides, you must have heard the gossip. She's shared between the Canford brothers, it's well known. She's everybody's woman——'

'I'm not, I'm not!' Bella shrieked, running halfway down the stairs. 'You're a louse, Malcolm Haddern. You're spreading lies and twisted rumours. If I h-had the strength I'd—I'd . . . Why d-don't you p-pick on one your own size?'

Her chattering teeth came through her words and she hugged her shivering body in an attempt to keep it still.

Reece appeared in the wide entrance hall, staring up. 'Bella! What the hell are you doing? You're not fit, get back to bed.'

'Yeah, *his* bed, where you came from.' Malcolm, joining his friend, nudged him.

Reece turned on him. 'Malc, get,' his jerking head indicated the door, 'before I pound you to a jelly. And if this goes any further than the walls of this building, I'll contact my lawyer, then proceed to savage your reputation, piece by piece, until no one, but no one will employ you again.'

Bella stared down at the two men.

Malcolm turned with pained astonishment to his friend, noting his implacability, his remorseless determination. His bounce left him, his brashness fled, and, with a feeble salute in Bella's direction, he slammed the door behind him.

Its echo reverberated, offending Bella's sensibilities, and she turned on Reece, feeling the need to purge herself of her remaining anger. Her agitation was obvious and he sprinted two at a time up to her level.

'You call yourself that man's *friend*,' she spat, deliberately backing away from his approach, 'and he says he's yours. So how do I know I can trust *you* any more than I can *him*?'

Reece's hands were on her shoulders and she jerked back, failing to shift his grip. 'I hate you as much as I hate him. Do you understand? I want to b-break that contract. I can't get away from you f-fast enough. I want to leave here. I want to go h-home...' But she didn't have a home! If she left Windham House, she would be *homeless*.

She stared at him, shattered by the sudden realisation, by the weakness that assailed her from nowhere, by the trembling of her body and her still chattering teeth.

She closed her eyes and swayed, gripping the banister rail. Arms enfolded her and gathered her shivering self into the sanctuary of a masculine embrace. Her head found his chest, her arms lifting to encounter his shoulders, her limp form sagging against his strength.

He swept her feet from the floor and carried her back to her bed, removing the robe she had pulled on and lifting the covers over her. But something inside her would not let him go, her arms holding on to him as they had never clung before.

'Don't—don't leave me,' she heard herself implore. 'I tried to sleep, but I kept getting these pictures, of the roof coming down, of the world caving in. Stay with me, Reece,' her eyes were fully open now and even in the semi-darkness she could see his anxiety, 'just—just until I get to sleep again. Then—then you can go.'

He stared down at her, and seemed to her to be using his eyes as X-rays, trying to penetrate to her inner mind, to comprehend her wishes.

'I have to go,' he smoothed her hair, 'but I'll be back. Ten minutes, hm?'

It seemed to Bella like ten hours, and she must have drifted off because she did not remember him getting in beside her, or the moment when he turned her from him and took her backwards into his arms.

'Sleep, now, Bella,' he was whispering. 'You're safe because I'm with you, do you hear?'

She nodded, sighed and slept. But even so, the terrifying images woke her, and she turned, overheated and frightened, towards the figure beside her.

He was awake at once—had he been asleep?—and held her to him, stroking her shoulders and arms, his soothing lips cool against her temples.

'Quiet now, Bella,' he murmured, 'everything's fine. Bella...oh, God, Bella,' he groaned, sliding her shoulder straps down and trailing her throat with hungry lips, 'you don't know what you're asking of me. How can I resist touching you? Bella,' he held her away, 'fight me, for God's sake, fight me. Tell me "no, Reece, no." Otherwise,' he said thickly, 'there'll be no turning back.'

Despite his warning, her arms clung. She could not let him go! Not only was he the one stable thing in her life at that moment, protecting her from the terrors of her nightmares, she wanted him, she loved him, the one thing she wanted most in the world was to belong to him...

'I can't, Reece, I can't fight you any more,' she whispered, her mouth dry, every particle of her leaping at his touch. 'Oh, Reece,' she felt his masculine arousal, felt sweet, heady sensations she had never experienced before sweeping over her, delighting in the exquisite aches and throbbing responses his mouth was drawing from her, 'I need you, don't you understand? I love you!'

With a smothered exclamation he let his mouth have its way, following his hands' path and making free with her breasts, his lips and teeth taking possession of her pouting nipples, and eliciting from her cries of pure pleasure and a pulsating, consuming desire.

His palms curved around the small swell of her stomach, stroking and teasing, sliding to secret hollows no other man had touched, pressing his hard thighs against her yielding softness, then using his leg to separate hers. He must have felt her readiness for him as he whispered hoarsely, 'I'm taking you, Bella. Say my name, say it out loud so you know without question who is lying with you.'

Why, she wondered dazedly, had he given such a command? Then she realised he still believed there had been others before him.

'Oh, Reece,' she murmured brokenly, 'don't you understand? I'm not——'

A cry broke from her as he entered her, and she heard his muffled exclamation. His pause was only momentary and the pleasure that he was giving her caused her to forget the sudden pain his intimate entry had inflicted.

She stroked his back, gripped his shoulders and parted her lips ever wider for his invading kiss. Arching towards him, she held back nothing, giving as well as taking, delighting in his thrusting possession, and the world itself receded as he carried her with him towards the explosion of ecstasy that made them indivisibly one.

He stayed beside her, the moistness of their skins mingling, their bodies still entwined. He took her again in the early hours, less gently this time, but with a flaring tenderness mixed in that brought tears to her eyes and lifted her to even greater heights of pleasure than before.

She woke to the daylight of midday, stretching her arm towards where he had lain, but his place was empty. Even so, she lay there smiling, revelling in the memory of his lovemaking, knowing he would return to her that night.

Her wounds had not miraculously healed but, she thought, there must have been a pain-killer blended in with his kisses and caresses, because they didn't hurt any more.

She took a shower and made her way down to the kitchen, knowing Reece had long gone to work. When she saw the note propped against her dishes on the breakfast counter, her heart began to hammer with foreboding.

'Bella,' it read, 'I've been called away to my parents' apartment in Spain. My father is ill, and my mother needs me. Jacqueline is coming, too. I shall be back as soon as the situation, whatever that may be, allows. In the meantime, don't go to work unless you feel really fit. I'll see you on my return. Then we must talk. Reece.'

Four days later, Bella returned to work. Polly greeted her with a joyous hug.

'It's done the trick,' she cried, 'that garden fête's put Food Basket at the top of the great hits of the century. We've been worked off our feet, Bella. The store manager let us have a couple of his assistants, otherwise we'd have been swamped. Isn't that great?' Polly checked herself. 'Sorry, Bella, I forgot to ask how you are. Have you got over that awful experience? Reece told us. He's away, but I expect you knew that, being his housekeeper.'

Bella pointed to the people lining up outside. 'Is that how it's been?'

'That's how it's been,' Polly repeated delightedly.

Bella's eyes shone. Her little shop was a success at last!

Ten days passed without news of Reece, but Bella told herself she wasn't worried. She missed him more than she had ever thought was possible, but she had his note tucked safely away beside her bed. On his return, it said, he would see her. And she him...

The shop was momentarily empty of customers and Bella was tidying the counter when Jacqueline walked in. They greeted each other joyfully, then Bella realised with a shock that, if she was back, her brother would surely have returned, too.

'How was your father?' Bella asked, strangely fearful of enquiring as to Reece's whereabouts.

'He's on the mend, thankfully,' Jacqueline answered, but something else seemed to be worrying her. 'What is it with you and Reece?' she asked at last.

Bella felt the colour flood into her face. 'What——' she cleared her throat '—what about Reece and me?'

Jacqueline's shoulders lifted and fell. 'Just something I heard. You're—um—still living at his place?'

Now Bella was really concerned. 'Of course. Why shouldn't I be?'

'Just wondered. Er——' She looked round, saw the customers gathering behind her for attention. 'You haven't seen my new place, have you, mine and Dick's? Come round tonight, Bella, I'll be on my own. We'll have a bite to eat and a girlish gossip? Sevenish. Must dash.' The customers good-humouredly moved aside for her.

Jacqueline's and Dick's house was a short distance from the town.

'The mat says "welcome",' Jacqueline said, opening the door. 'Before we eat, I'll show you over our future domain. It'll only take a few minutes, unlike Reece's place. A couple of rooms are furnished, that's all,' she explained as they moved around the small house.

The meal was light, but satisfying and, having talked throughout without stopping, Jacqueline, after clearing the dishes, seemed unexpectedly hesitant.

'Are you,' she enquired slowly, 'thinking of giving up your job as Reece's housekeeper?'

Bella's spirits came crashing from the heights to which they had risen after the night of lovemaking that she had shared with Reece. 'Not at present,' she answered carefully.

'Mm. Which means it's probably just another horrid rumour. I'll try and explain.' Jacqueline seemed reluctant to continue, and appeared to be choosing her words. 'Reece flew back with me. When I asked if he was going home, he said "no". But he didn't tell me where he would be staying.'

Bella's clasped hands had grown moist, her breathing becoming a little difficult to control.

'I happened to meet Marguerite Hunter-Parkes and she told me... Bella, love, you're not going to like this.' Her hand reached out across the sofa and squeezed Bella's. 'Marguerite told me he's staying with her father. And,' she took a deep breath, 'she knows for certain that he's interviewed someone for the post of housekeeper at Windham House. Apparently, the woman went to her father's place in Hampstead for the interview. A pleasant middle-aged lady, Marguerite said, not very tall, Scottish accent.'

'I—I can't believe it!' Bella exclaimed, unable to hide her dismay.

'You mean Reece didn't even have the courtesy, let alone the consideration, to let you know? I could slaughter my brother!' After a moment's thought, she said, 'You signed and exchanged contracts, didn't you?'

Bella nodded stiffly. 'Three months' notice on either side. But if he wants to replace me, I wouldn't hang around. Jacqueline,' she attempted to control the wobble in her voice, 'do you think that means he wants me out of Food Basket, too?'

'You'd be quite entitled to take him to court on both counts. Don't spare him, pal, he isn't sparing you.' The telephone rang and Jacqueline sprang at it. 'Dick darling? I've missed you. It's been all of two hours since we parted. Yes, Bella's with me. Oh, dear, you're driving her away. She's collecting her things. Stay,' Jacqueline urged, covering the mouthpiece, but Bella shook her head.

As she fastened her safety-belt, Bella thanked her friend for everything. 'Well,' her voice wobbled again, 'you know what I mean.'

Jacqueline squeezed Bella's shoulder. 'Nothing to thank me for, really, is there?' She stood back, waving.

'I've called you, Jimmy,' Bella said into the telephone, 'to ask a favour. Do you remember that some time ago you told me your mother would take me in if ever I found myself homeless? Well, Jimmy, I'm about to be made...' To her horror, she burst into tears.

'Hey, Bella love, what's wrong? Polly's at her parents' house, so I'll come over. Give me ten minutes.'

He was prompt and filled with concern when he saw Bella's tear-stained face. 'Tell me all about it,' he invited.

It all came pouring out. 'Reece is actually going to replace me without telling me first!' she finished bewilderedly. 'I can hardly believe it's true, but according to

Jacqueline, who sees no reason to disbelieve what Marguerite told her, it is.'

'You want to leave here tonight? I can take you and your things in my van, if you like. I asked my mother on my way out and she said of course you could stay with her and Dad.'

'That's very good of her, but I've only just started packing, and there's lots more to do. Anyway, I can drive myself there. I've still got my old car, thanks to you and Vernon and Throttle Garage.'

She managed a tearful smile and, after a cup of tea and a reassuring hug, he left her to finish her packing.

She had, in fact, told Jimmy only half the story. The rest she had kept strictly to herself. No one would ever hear from her how close to Reece she had once been, how, in her dreams, she still felt his lips on hers, his hands on her skin and, because it was a dream, a look of love in his eyes.

She ran upstairs, pulling clothes out of the wardrobes and drawers and thrusting them without much order into her suitcases.

It must have been only minutes after Jimmy had left that the front door swung open, its ancient hinges creaking a warning message. Bella stopped in her tracks, hand to her mouth. Reece had come home!

'Bella! *Bella*!' His voice carried around the house, commanding, angry. His feet carried him inexorably up the stairs, then he was at her door, staring at her, then at the suitcases.

His mouth set in a formidable line, his hands slid into his pockets, his broad shoulders finding a misleadingly casual perch against the door-frame.

'Leaving, are you?' he enquired silkily. 'Eloping with James Canford, then? Been making plans? And don't try telling me he hasn't been here, because I passed him in the drive.'

'No to both your questions,' she threw back, eyes brilliant and challenging, 'just going to live in his house.'

Reece's upper lip drew back, then he snapped his teeth together. 'So you're finally moving in with him. Sharing his double bed at last.'

Why should she tell this man she thought she loved, yet whom she told herself she now hated with a fierce hatred, the truth about how things stood between herself and Jimmy Canford?

'Jimmy knows how I feel about him.'

'He does, eh? Great for him.' Reece straightened and advanced into the room. His breathing was deep and slow, his eyes sizing her up like a prowling predator assessing potential prey for a reasonable meal. 'And do you know how *I* feel about *you*?'

'Yes. You—you look as though you could throttle me.' She flung back her head. 'Yet I'm not the one who's in the process of tearing up that contract we both signed. *You* are. You're the one who's already interviewed my replacement as your housekeeper.'

He frowned, then appeared to comprehend. 'I have, have I?'

'Yes, you have. Jacqueline told me. Marguerite Hunter-Parkes told her. She saw the lady in question at her father's house in London. You—you've been staying there,' she accused, 'yet you told me you would see me when you returned. It says so in your note.' She produced it from the back of a drawer.

Reece's eyebrows lifted non-committally. 'All right, so I'm seeing you. Now. And if you want to know why I stayed with Marguerite's father, it's because I flew into a London airport and thought I'd get some business I had with him out of the way before I drove back to

Windhamleigh. And I haven't appointed anyone in your place as my housekeeper. Yet.'

It was that one small word and the threat it contained that infuriated her. 'So it'll help you, won't it, if I pack up and go? OK,' with a false airiness, 'tear up that contract. See if I m-mind.' She cursed her voice for faltering. 'And if you don't, *I* will.'

'And if you do, I shall sue you for breach of that contract. Relentlessly, squeezing the last penny out of you.' He said the words so coldly, so distinctly, Bella halted her packing and stared at him.

'You wouldn't.'

'Want to try me?' He made to reach for the phone, then paused. 'Too late to catch my solicitor at his office. But leave me your address—that is, Canford's address— won't you, so that the necessary papers can be served on you?'

Bella blanched with anger. 'Deny you interviewed someone for my job while I still occupied it,' she challenged, her voice high. Oh, please, she pleaded silently, say you didn't, say the rumour was wrong.

'OK, so I interviewed a woman for the job of housekeeper in this house.'

Shaking at the admission, she took up his note—the note she had cherished and had read every night in his absence—and tore it to pieces, throwing them at him.

'You are the most unscrupulous, vindictive man,' she cried, 'I've ever had the misfortune to meet. You—you p-pretended to like me enough to m-make love to me, t-treated me like a—a cheap little tramp, then calmly walked out as if nothing had h-happened. S-suppose I'm pregnant as a result?'

'You won't be. I took good care of that.' His eyes were in shadow, his arms folded across his chest, as remote from her as the summit of Everest. And as cold.

He came to sudden, frightening life, but the heat that emanated from him was not warm, but searing and devouring. He seized her shoulders and the contact almost burned her skin.

'You, my little spitfire, allowed me to make love to you, all the while fantasising that it was Canford you were lying with. All right, so you obediently repeated my name when I told you to, but for you it was the wrong name, wasn't it, the *wrong man*?'

'No, not true! All the time I knew it was you.'

He put her from him. 'Then why are you running *to* him *from* me?'

'I'm not. It's his parents' house I'm going to. He and Vernon have got their own place nearby.'

'You're going there, prior to marrying him?'

'No,' she whispered. Her legs gave way and she sank on to the bed. 'You win,' she said, closing her eyes, 'I'll stay for the three months I agreed to in that contract.' Her eyes fluttered open. 'And for your information as my *employer*, I'm not going to marry anybody.'

'If that's so, what was Jimmy Canford doing kissing you at the fête?'

'It was a goodbye gesture. I'd as good as told him I didn't return his feelings. It's Polly he's beginning to notice, and I think she likes him. Which is just fine by me. Tonight he was here to comfort me because I was—upset. About you making arrangements to replace me without telling me. Now, will you please go?'

There was a long and puzzling pause. 'Never.'

Her head lifted sharply at his subtle tone change. If her expression mirrored her feelings for him, her soaring hope that he might mean what his tone and eyes implied, then she didn't care any more. She didn't hate this man. She loved him so much that, even if he intended to dismiss her from his life, she didn't care if he guessed how she felt about him.

'Please, tell me what you mean,' she pleaded.

'What I say, Isabella.' Lifting her to her feet, he pulled her close. His eyes were like twin suns, dazzling her, giving rise to such hopes in her heart she thought it might burst within her.

'So,' his jaw thrust forward, 'you're not going to marry *anyone*? OK by me, my lovely Bella, just as long as you live with me exclusively for the rest of our lives.' His mouth came up against hers and the pressure of it pushed back her head until her lips parted, allowing him access to its honeyed moistness.

After a long time, raising his head, he said against her lips, 'But it might be better for the children we're going to have if you married me and wore my ring. Hm?'

'Marry you?' She was laughing and crying, and beside herself with happiness. 'I know I love you more than words can say, but——'

'For pity's sake, Bella,' he groaned, 'stop opposing me, challenging me, or I'll take you here and now.'

'But how, I was going to say,' she whispered, her eyes sparkling, 'how do I know that *you* love *me*?'

'She's asking me,' he growled, snapping his teeth, 'she's inviting me, *provoking* me. So I'll show you, little temptress, I'll demonstrate not only that I love you, but just *how much* I love you.' He held her away. 'But first tell me you'll marry me.'

'I'll marry you,' she whispered breathlessly.

'Now, Bella Harrison,' he commanded, 'remove all barriers to your husband-to-be.' He began the process himself, then watched with narrowed male eyes as she obeyed his command. 'All of them, every seductive, frilly piece. I want to see my lovely fiancée in all her beauty.' She finally stood before him, every garment gone.

Slowly, eyes lingering on her creamy skin and enticing curves, he started removing his own clothes, telling her in the end to finish the job, which she shyly did. Then he opened her arms wide, letting his gaze meander over her, uncaring that she trembled under his minute regard.

'Clear the bed of your belongings, Isabella,' he said huskily, watching as she did so, 'you're not going anywhere else but here. Understand?'

Then he swooped, lifting her high until she squealed and writhed against the grasp of his upraised hands, dropping her at last on to the covers, falling with her, covering her body with his.

He let her feel all of his potent maleness, then drew on to his side, stroking her tingling, quivering skin, first with his eyes, then with the pads of his fingertips, making trails all over her. He watched her small, leaping responses, seeing the glow in her eyes deepen to an intense and pleading desire.

'*Ma belle* Bella,' he murmured huskily, 'beautiful in every way.' He rolled on to her, taking charge of her mouth and imprisoning her hands above her head. She wriggled and twisted under the impact of his muscled body, aching with sweet pain as the friction between their heated skins aroused in her a desperate need for the total fulfilment which only he in the whole world could give her.

'Bella, Bella,' he murmured thickly, 'stop fighting me. Let all your feelings go and let yourself go with them.'

She laughed chokily. 'It wasn't so long ago, darling, that you told me to fight you. Now you're——'

'Stop talking, lady.' His mouth, seeking and tasting the sweetness within hers, saw to it that she did. Then his lips embarked on a voyage of discovery, moving down, down over her body, savouring every inch of her smooth, silky skin, his tongue rousing to hammering life pulses all over her that she never knew she had. When his lips moved lower to invade her most intimate places, she was on fire for him and the very essence of her reached out to him for the ultimate and joyous satisfaction that he seemed tormentingly to be withholding from her.

When she thought she could stand it no longer, when his erotic caresses created in her such an aching need that her fingertips dug deeply into the taut muscles of his arms, she cried out, 'I surrender, darling, I love you too much ever to fight you again.'

At which confession, one that he seemed to have been intent on drawing from her, she heard his exultant laugh. Then he took her, possessing her with so much passion that she melted into him, feeling him carry her with him to heights of such ecstasy that she cried out his name, telling him over and over again how much she loved him.

'I've loved *you*,' he reminisced, kissing her nose and then her lips as, much later, they reclined in each other's arms on Reece's sofa, 'since you were a teenager with flashing eyes behind the counter of Harrison's Food Fare.'

'But, Reece!' she exclaimed. 'The way you used to look at me—yes, I noticed, and you know I noticed,' she smoothed away his frown, 'so you needn't pretend to look surprised—I thought you—well, were being deliberately lustful just to annoy me. Because I was only a girl from the other end of the town.'

'I, madam,' he pretended to push her off him, 'should spank you for that. Of course lust was mixed up in it— the look, I mean—but love was there, too. No woman, before or since, has ever come up to Isabella Harrison in my eyes.'

'Did you ever believe the rumours about me?'

'About your playing fast and loose with the Canford brothers? Do you really think, Bella, that I'm such a poor judge of character that, in the end, I couldn't work the truth out for myself?'

'Meaning that, at first, you had your doubts?'

He gave a small shrug. 'You must admit that, in going around with both of them, you provided evidence enough for some people to jump to that conclusion.' For a while they kissed, then he commented with a provoking smile, 'Do you realise, Miss Harrison, that you've finally and irrevocably come over to the "enemy"? To the so-called "other side of the town"?'

'Are you implying that I've therefore gone back on my principles?' she asked indignantly.

'In reality, principles don't enter into it. It was simply an imaginary line which you and your contemporaries drew between the older part and the new.' He shifted her into a more comfortable and closer position. 'I'll tell you a secret. My parents—did Jacqueline ever tell you?— rarely showed either of us much affection, let alone love. You don't know how often I wanted to follow my sister and cross your "dividing line" into *your* side of town.'

'You did?'

'I did. Nor do you know how often I envied Jacqueline her access to it—to you, to your particular brand of warmth, to your parents' welcome and loving kindness.'

'So why didn't you, darling?' she asked softly.

'Because I thought you might hate me even more for intruding into your world. And that you might run the other way.'

'There's still something I don't understand.' He tipped her chin, looking into her eyes and encouraging her to go on. 'Why did you interview that lady for the post of housekeeper?'

He laughed. 'I wondered when that was coming. Mrs Campbell's her name. A friend of hers knew an acquaintance of mine who told her that, since my sister was getting married, she was sure I'd soon be in need of a housekeeper. So, since she was in London, she rang the only number that friend of mine had—Jacqueline's, who gave her Marguerite's number, who passed her on to her father's house where she knew I was staying.'

'And you interviewed her? Why?'

'Don't sound so hurt, my love. I was going to acquire a wife myself, was I not?' Those imperious eyebrows lifted, but the eyes were warm.

'Well, of all the arrogant... How did you know I'd say yes?'

'How did I——? How do you think? After leaving your bed, after our passionate night together, what else do you think I had in mind regarding your beautiful self but marriage? I thought that one day in the not-so-distant future Mrs Campbell might come in very useful—as *our* housekeeper. Yes?'

'Oh, yes, Reece darling,' she breathed. 'Just one more thing. What,' she said in a small voice, playing with the buttons on his knitted shirt, 'about Marguerite?'

'You mean where does she fit into my life?' His shrug was dismissive. 'I hold shares in her business, which means there'll continue to be some contact between us.'

'Only—only on business?' Bella asked uncertainly.

He laughed. 'What else do you think, my love? No other woman has ever meant, nor will ever mean, as much to me as you do. Anyway, whatever might have been between Marguerite and myself was over long ago.'

With which reply Bella was entirely content.

'I'll never forget, darling,' she told him, 'how you helped me when I was in trouble after the inspector's report on Food Fare, and how wonderful it was of you to do what you did—buy the business and give me Bella's Food Basket. At the time, I didn't know how to thank you.'

'But now you do.'

She looked up and caught the anticipatory glint in his eyes. She wrinkled her nose and whispered with a bright, provocative glance, 'I don't know what you mean.'

'No?' There was a world of meaning in the question as he lifted her into his arms, swinging her towards the stairs and striding up them.

'I'll show you, beloved,' he said.

HARLEQUIN  PRESENTS®

BARBARY WHARF

**An exciting six-book series, one title per month
beginning in October, by bestselling author**

Set in the glamorous and fast-paced world of international
journalism, BARBARY WHARF will take you from the
Sentinel's hectic newsroom to the most thrilling cities in the
world. You'll meet media tycoon Nick Caspian and his
adversary Gina Tyrrell, whose dramatic story of passion and
heartache develops throughout the six-book series.

In book one, BESIEGED (#1498), you'll also meet Hazel and
Piet. Hazel's always had a good word to say about everyone.
Well, almost. She just can't stand Piet Van Leyden, Nick's
chief architect and one of the most arrogant know-it-alls she's
ever met! As far as Hazel's concerned, Piet's a twentieth-
century warrior, and she's the one being besieged!

Don't miss the sparks in the first BARBARY WHARF
book, BESIEGED (#1498), available in October from
Harlequin Presents.

BARB-S

JAYNE ANN KRENTZ

A two-part epic tale from one of today's most popular romance novelists!

Dreams
Parts One & Two

The warrior died at her feet, his blood running out of the cave entrance and mingling with the waterfall. With his last breath he cursed the woman— told her that her spirit would remain chained in the cave forever until a child was created and born there....

So goes the ancient legend of the Chained Lady and the curse that bound her throughout the ages—until destiny brought Diana Prentice and Colby Savager together under the influence of forces beyond their understanding. Suddenly they were both haunted by dreams that linked past and present, while their waking hours were filled with danger. Only when Colby, Diana's modern-day warrior, learned to love, could those dark forces be vanquished. Only then could Diana set the Chained Lady free....

**Available in September
wherever Harlequin books are sold.**

JK92

HARLEQUIN
Romance®

HARLEQUIN ROMANCE IS BETTING ON LOVE!

And The Bridal Collection's
September title is a sure bet.

JACK OF HEARTS (#3218)
by Heather Allison

THE BRIDAL COLLECTION

THE BRIDE played her part.
THE GROOM played for keeps.
THEIR WEDDING was in the cards!

Available in August in
THE BRIDAL COLLECTION:

THE BEST-MADE PLANS (#3214)
by Leigh Michaels

Harlequin Romance

Wherever Harlequin
books are sold.

WELCOME TO

The quintessential small town, where everyone knows everybody else!

Finally, books that capture the pleasure of tuning in to your favorite TV show!

GREAT READING...GREAT SAVINGS...AND A FABULOUS FREE GIFT!

Each book set in Tyler is a self-contained love story; together, the twelve novels stitch the fabric of the community. The covers honor the old American tradition of quilting; each cover depicts a patch of the large Tyler quilt.

With Tyler you can receive a fabulous gift, ABSOLUTELY FREE, by collecting proofs-of-purchase found in each Tyler book. And use our special Tyler coupons to save on your next TYLER book purchase.

Join your friends at Tyler for the seventh book, ARROWPOINT by Suzanne Ellison,
available in September.

Rumors fly about the death at the old lodge! What happens when Renata Meyer finds an ancient Indian sitting cross-legged on her lawn?
